Life in Parallel

Sadiq Awal

Published in Australia by Sid Harta Books & Print Pty Ltd,
ABN: 34632585293
23 Stirling Crescent, Glen Waverley, Victoria 3150 Australia
Telephone: +61 3 9560 9920, Facsimile: +61 3 9545 1742
E-mail: author@sidharta.com.au

First published in Australia 2023
This edition published 2023
Copyright © Sadiq Awal 2023

Cover design, typesetting: WorkingType (www.workingtype.com.au)

ISBN: 978-1-922958-28-0

About the Author

Sadiq Awal describes himself as a real-life storyteller. Born and raised in Bangladesh, he began his career as a marine scientist before joining a national university. Since 1998 he and his family have lived in Melbourne where he works as a lecturer in environmental science. He completed his PhD at Deakin University, Victoria Australia. He has published several books and articles in Bengali. *Life in Parallel* is his first English novel.

Throughout my life, my mother, Anwara Begum, has been a source of love and unconditional support.

Although she is no longer in this world, I am pretty sure she has been watching me each and every moment from heaven awaiting my arrival.

Acknowledgements

Creating a book out of an idea is not as easy as many might think. It is both challenging and rewarding on so many levels. This book would not have been as readable as it is without the help of Tony Berry and Marc Campobasso.

It was Marc Campobasso, one of my favourite students, who unceasingly edited and restructured my thoughts and helped me discipline them. He guided me in blasting through the substantial barrier between my unwieldy early sketches to create something that resembled a book from my early and much too long and raw first draft.

Another major contributor to the writing process was my editor, Tony Berry. It would not have been possible for me to accomplish my work without his continuous support and vision. The editorial guidance, insights and ongoing support Tony provided to help me bring my stories to life will remain in my heart forever.

Merina Begum, my wife and constant source of support and inspiration, has my greatest appreciation. Our daughters, Sabrina and Samiyah, have shown admirable understanding and sacrifice in supporting my writing.

Finally, I would like to acknowledge with gratitude, the ongoing support and love of my youngest sister, Mahfuza Sultana, who has been a constant inspiration to me throughout my career.

Arif Ahmed lay rigid and frozen on a table that felt too small for him. Every cell in his body hummed with the acute awareness of being in an unfamiliar place. It took all his concentration to try to suppress the backlog of uncontrolled movements he felt building in his body and that he feared would spill out at any moment.

He lay on his stomach with his arms awkwardly by his side. A small bead of sweat formed on his brow and grew larger and cooler, slipping down the bridge of his nose as gravity took over. As he peered through the small hole in the bottom of the table, the drop of sweat fell to the tiles below. He closed his eyes slowly.

He felt a swell of anxiety as the hands hovered above his shoulders as he lost himself in the darkness behind his eyelids. He felt more relaxed as the hands climbed his neck and into his hair. Suddenly he felt as if he was being thrown backward in time.

When he was a child, his maa always waited beside his bed when he awoke with a fever dream.

A wave of drowsy calm came over him as she stroked his hair in a gentle whisper. She would ask him to lift his heavy little head so she could cover the pillow with a thin, plastic-covered sheet and dab his forehead with cold water from a small teapot. As his maa stroked his hair in hypnotic circular strokes, he drifted off to sleep as her other hand caressed his hair.

'Please roll over, sir,' the young woman said, arousing him from his daydream.

He struggled to roll over on the narrow massage table, but at least he could wear his glasses again. Reaching for the bedside table, he placed them back on his face. Finally, he was able to see again.

When he first entered the massage room through the parted white sheet, all he could see was the massage table, covered in another white sheet, and the small bedside table from which he had retrieved his glasses. A lumpy white cushion adorned an armless, iron-framed chair.

He could see his shirt propped over the back of it and began to worry that the fabric would absorb the smell of incense and massage oil that surrounded him.

He had almost refused to enter the parlour because of the overwhelming smell and now his eyes were irritated by all the smoke and incense dust.

Candlelight flickered in the corner of the room where a statue of Buddha held incense sticks that were masking the smell of something deeper, darker and more unpleasant.

Arif imagined himself passing out and suffocating as the masseuse worked around his shoulders and neck. Perhaps his organs would be harvested? He had heard of such things. At first, when the masseuse asked him to take off his shirt, he was taken aback.

Arif never took off his shirt. He didn't even take it off in front of Nira, his dear wife.

'There is no need for me to take my shirt off. I only need a head and neck massage,' Arif pleaded slightly.

'No. You'll ruin it. Too much oil. Please take it off or no massage.' She stood with arms folded, staring straight ahead. Arif found it difficult to look into her face.

It was the first time he had been inside a massage parlour and he wasn't comfortable with strangers buffing his naked skin. But Arif had come too far out of his comfort zone to turn back. The shirt he handed her was undone. While hunching over and withdrawing, his torso trembled slightly.

The masseuse had made it to the centre of his forehead and her thumbs were pushing the thick slick of oil outwards towards his temples. As the skin stretched on his forehead, he looked at her face for the first time and realised that she was young and attractive, but he couldn't guess her age.

'What's your name?' he asked.

'Nicole.'

'How long have you been in Australia?'

'Not long. Only nine months or so. I still feel like a stranger in this country.'

She picked up a large ceramic bowl from the floor and turned towards the exit, leaving Arif puzzled as he watched her disappear through the drapes.

He noticed a printed sign on the wall. The large bold font read, 'Please be quiet. Enjoy the massage while allowing other customers to enjoy their massages as well.'

The girl returned through the curtain. The bowl she was holding was now tracking steam through the air in front of her. Two small white towels were draped over the insides of her elbows.

'Please take off your glasses,' she said as she dipped one of the towels in the bowl of steaming liquid. Arif removed them and placed them on the bedside table.

'Now close your eyes,' she instructed, and he did.

Arif sighed as she placed the hot towels over his eyelids. She applied a slight pressure with one hand while the other hand kept working the muscles in his scalp. Now he was curious.

'Where did you learn how to massage?' Arif asked gently.

'My boss, the owner of this shop, trained me before I started working,' she said.

'And what were you doing before this?'

'I graduated in mathematics from a university in my country before I moved here. I'm here to study English,' she said.

Arif tried to sit up, struck by a mix of surprise and interest, but she had him held firmly by his earlobes.

'You graduated in mathematics?' His amazement was obvious.

Arif had a bittersweet relationship with mathematics. In primary school he was confident with the subject and regularly got good grades. But things changed when his father died suddenly, leaving his mother – Maa, as they called her – to look after him and his numerous siblings.

From an early age, Bhaijan, his eldest brother, sacrificed much for the family. He worked in the capital, sending most of his weekly pay cheques to Maa, who could afford a small apartment with two bedrooms. To gain access to better schools and other facilities, the children moved to a small town away from their father's village. His mother expected two things from her children. First, that they applied themselves wholeheartedly and took advantage of every opportunity to expand their education; and second that they honoured Bhai for his sacrifices. Getting bad grades would have meant Arif had failed on both counts, but he struggled in high school without the guidance of his older brother or father.

Arif found algebra, trigonometry and geometry extremely difficult and alien to him. Teachers seemed unable or unwilling to explain the concepts clearly, and due to the overwhelming amount of homework he was assigned, he found himself left hopelessly behind.

In those days, things were different, he thought. The canes and other humiliations he endured every day were in stark contrast to today when students receive remedial help to catch up. The humiliations he had suffered as a student still made him feel like a failure today, even as a professor.

'Thanks Nicole, please finish up. I'd like to leave now,' he said.

The girl looked at him, an eyebrow raised quizzically, a scowl travelling across her face.

'You've paid for one hour. You still have half an hour left.'

Arif shrugged. 'Sorry, I have got to go. What can I say?'

The masseuse crouched down close over Arif's splayed body. He could smell her breath and the sweat on her neck.

'Do you want a little more than a massage?' Her voice was now low and husky.

'More than massage?' he asked and gulped the air. 'What is more …?'

Nicole interrupted him by putting her hand on the fly of his pants. He clutched her hand and pushed it away.

'No, no,' he said, quickly. 'I have no need for that.'

The girl took half a step backwards and tilted her head, curious.

'Sorry,' she said, surprised. 'I thought you'd want that. Most of the men who come here want that.'

Arif looked at her as he adjusted his glasses.

'How did you get here, to this parlour in Australia?' he asked.

Nicole shrugged and looked away. Maybe he had offended her. He thought he detected a line of annoyance on her forehead.

'Are you annoyed with me?'

'I'm not annoyed,' Nicole assured him. 'But you're making me feel uncomfortable.'

'I am so sorry,' said Arif. 'I don't know why I asked like that. I guess I feel comfortable talking to you. I don't talk much outside of school. Teaching students is like carrying on an unremitting conversation. I usually don't feel like talking for the rest of the day.'

'Are you a teacher?' Nicole tilted her head, questioning.

He gave a humble smile. 'Yes, I am.'

'Where do you teach?'

'I teach at a university,' he answered, looking up at her.

'You're a university lecturer?'

Arif smiled at her and nodded.

'What subject do you teach?'

For the first time Arif felt that she was looking at him and not through him. Until this moment she had been withdrawn and distant.

'I teach chemistry, water chemistry. Have you studied chemistry before?'

'Not since high school. As an undergraduate, I took physics and mathematics.' She paused for a while, before continuing, 'Look, we can keep talking but we need to keep our voices low. My boss doesn't like us talking with customers.'

Arif nodded, still curious. 'Tell me how you found this massage work.

'There was no other work available. I had no other options. My agent offered me this or be a café waitress. But that can be awfully long hours for not much money. I earn more here. Besides, my English is still not particularly good, so...'

'No, it's good,' said Arif. 'You speak very good English.'

'Thank you,' she smiled.

'Call me Arif,' he said.

'I'll call you Professor Arif,' she said, with a hint of flirtation.

Arif liked that, despite his better judgement. He smiled back.

'I've come to Australia to learn English at college, so I appreciate your compliment,' she said. 'It should take me two years to finish the course.'

'And what are your plans after that?'

'I don't know what I'll do yet. It all depends on whether I get an opportunity to apply for Australian residency,' she replied. 'My real name is not Nicole.'

'What's your real name?'

'Yameli.'

'Hi Amelia,' said Arif, mishearing her name.

The young woman laughed. 'Lots of people back home used to call me Amelia as well.'

She tilted her head and raised her eyebrows for a moment, a bemused smile on her face.

'Do you mind if I call you Amelia? I like that name,' said Arif.

'Sure, why not? A rose by any other name…' she replied.

'Ah, you know Western literature?'

'Everyone knows Shakespeare,' she said. 'I'm not just a masseuse.

Arif reached his hand towards the armchair where his shirt was draped over the top. He turned to Amelia. 'Please could I have my shirt back? Maybe a towel to get some oil off my shoulders as well.'

'Of course.'

She picked up the ceramic bowl, which was no longer steaming, and walked out the door. When she returned a minute later Arif had already peeled himself from the massage table and was tapping his foot nervously.

'Please get back on the table, professor,' she said firmly. 'I need you to lie on your back.'

'I've never been in a massage parlour before. In fact, I've never even had a real massage,' he said, awkwardly dragging his body across the table on his back.

'Why today then?' asked Amelia chirpily as she worked the hot towel over his upper torso.

'I don't know. I drive past here almost every day. One time my car was stopped at the traffic lights in front, and I saw you... or maybe another girl, entering. Whoever it was, she reminded me of my students, and because the person reminded me of the students, and I've heard so many bad things about these places, I became curious about what happens here. My curiosity is almost too strong for me sometimes, stronger than my good judgement.'

He tilted his head forward.

'That means you came just to see me,' said Amelia. '... or the other girl.' She rolled her eyes and smirked in disbelief.

'Not only to see you, but also to see what happens in a massage parlour. I don't get any relief from my obsessive curiosity until I find answers.' He smiled, 'By the way, I didn't enjoy the massage.'

They both laughed out loud, then abruptly stopped. Arif looked up at the sign: BE QUIET.

'I knew that already,' Amelia whispered. 'When I was rubbing and kneading your neck and shoulders, you weren't comfortable at all. You were squirming like an eel. Anyway, massage time is over. Here's your shirt.'

Arif took it from her and got down off the table.

'Thank you,' he said.

He instinctively turned around to put his shirt on and felt embarrassed by his superfluous modesty.

'How do you say goodbye in your language?' he asked her as he stood up.

'*Sawasdee krab*,' she answered, lifting her hand into a wave.

'*Sawasdee krab*,' said Arif, lifting his hand, mirroring her actions and words. 'What days do you work here?'

'Tuesday and Thursday,' she replied. '*Sawasdee krab*.'

'*Sawasdee krab*,' said Arif, instantly feeling he had overstayed his welcome.

Arif left through the discrete exit that led to the rear carpark. A tinted glass door was obstructed by a beaded string curtain that jangled like discordant wind chimes when he pushed his way through. It dragged over him like glass jellyfish tentacles. .

He fumbled in his pocket for the button that unlocked his car, relieved to be away from the aromatic stench and out in the fresh air.

It was drizzling and he heard the splash of car tyres on the main road beyond. He walked across the wet bitumen, trying not to splash water on to the legs of his trousers. Only then did he realise he had forgotten to offer Amelia anything in the way of a tip. He decided he needed to return there another day.

2

An early morning ray of sunlight illuminated the kitchen as Arif walked in and found Nira finishing breakfast. Smiles spread across their faces as their eyes met.

'Good morning,' he greeted his wife.

'Good morning, Arif,' Nira replied. She walked towards him and began ruffling the collar of his shirt. 'This is a very colourful shirt,' she remarked.

'Thanks, Nira. I got it last year at that conference in Honolulu. The organisers gave one to all the delegates. You don't remember, do you?' He paused for a moment noting Nira's smug smile and steadfast gaze.

'Does it seem weird how I look?' ' he asked.

'Nope, you don't look odd at all. It's just that your shirt is loud, very loud, more suitable for a younger person.'

'Thanks, Nira,' he huffed, before turning to walk out the door. 'This old man needs to change his shirt.'

'You don't have to change. I'm sure your students will like it.'

'No, no. I am taking it off. I might be a little late today, but that's okay,' he insisted.

He took one hand off the button on his shirt and walked towards the bedroom. Nira followed close behind.

'I hope I haven't upset you before work,' she said, entering the bedroom.

'Why would I be upset over a shirt?'

'Well, I wasn't exactly complimentary. It would be a great shirt for a picnic or a barbecue ...'

Arif cut her off mid-sentence. 'Yes, my dear, you are right. Clothing isn't my strong suit. Fashion is not something I understand. Seems like I was about to present a lecture looking like a stand-up comedian.'

'I could choose another shirt for you ... that would be fun,' Nira said.

'Well... yeah. Okay.' Arif nodded his agreement.

She stepped into the walk-in wardrobe and immediately pulled out a long sleeved cream shirt and began unbuttoning it while Arif took off the colourful one.

'Wear this, it suits you better.'

While Nira stood in front of the mirror, she extended one of the sleeves and Arif reached through it. She moved behind him and helped him with the other arm. As she stood in front of him to do up his buttons, she pressed herself closer and closer to his torso until his shirt was fully fastened. She stepped back to assess her choice of shirt.

'Wow, Arif. Now you look like a smart and scholastic professor.'

Jokingly, he asked her, 'What is a smart professor? And what is a scholastic professor? Surely all professors are scholastic in some way. The context determines whether or not we are smart.'

'For you, it's just your job title, but for me, it's much more.' Nira felt proud of her husband's position as a professor. 'It makes me proud every time I think about it.'

Using his finger, Arif stretched the skin beneath his eye downward. 'Could you please look at my right eye, Nira? There must be something in there, it's galling, I can't see properly,' he said in sudden desperation.

Worried, Nira approached closer, a holding Arif's chest firmly while searching for dirt in his lower and upper eyelids. With his arms around Nira's body and his chest pressed tightly against her, Arif smiled mischievously and held her even tighter.

3

Nira and Arif had been married for twenty-five years. Her personality was always cheerful and happy, and she was always smiling. She smiled beautifully. Nira's eyes also smiled and looking at her eyes alone was enough to reveal that she was smiling. There was no excess fat on her body. In addition to keeping everything neat and clean, she was very organised. In their house, there was no dirt or dust to be found. And despite its size, the furniture, televisions, refrigerators and flooring were all clean. Everything appeared to be polished to a high gloss.

While they were building the house, Arif told Nira, 'Don't ask me how big it will be, what kind of kitchen it will be, how big the garage will be, or what kind of front door it will have. It's all up to you.'

Nira had performed her duties effectively. She had applied a great amount of effort. Her dream had always been to have a large kitchen like this — plenty of room to include a built-in pantry, spice rack and an extra-large dining area. All the jars in the spice rack had tightly sealed lids, none were open or loose. All were labelled to show the contents. Neatly folded and clean kitchen towels hung over the handrail above the spacious oven top.

Arif himself was a very tidy person. Cleanliness and neatness were important to him. During his university years, he lived in a student hostel. There were three separate beds in the room that he shared with two roommates. It was his habit to spread his bed linen nicely — pillows and quilt were neatly arranged next to his bed. The stationery and books were kept well organised.

He was an early riser and every day he swept and cleaned the whole room. In many student rooms, a long rope was used as the line for drying clothes but Arif used clothes lines on the hostel roof instead.

After his father died, Arif was sent by Maa to live with his sister's family in a small town near their village. The sister, Apa, lived with her husband (whom Arif called Bhai) and their two children: Lilly, a three-year-old girl, and Joy, an eighteen-month-old boy. Bhai earned meagre wages as an administrative clerk at a private office. Instead of seeking to supplement his income, Bhai devoted himself to unpaid, charitable work, which meant money was always tight.

Apa bought all their non-perishable groceries at the beginning of every month, and guests were a burden on their supplies. In the afternoons, Apa would make homemade flatbread to serve with dinner as rice was much more expensive at the market than flour and the family couldn't afford rice for both meals. At each meal, two rotis would be given to the children and three to the adults. When things were good, they would eat their roti with eggplant, potato and cauliflower curries. In times of shortage, they served green papaya curry because it was cheap and readily available. After every dinner, Apa served everyone a piece of confectionery made of sugarcane juice or dried dates.

Apa served Bhai and Arif rice and vegetable curries in the morning. At 8 am, Bhai left for work. Arif walked to school with a full stomach, but would soon be hungry again.

During recess, other children often bought tiffin from the cafeteria, such as peanuts, pickled cucumbers, olives, mango chutney, berry chutney, and other treats that Arif enjoyed. While the other children ate ice cream off wooden sticks, Arif pumped cold water from the courtyard well and played under the mango trees while they ate.

He often sat with his back to a tree, watching the others play. Despite not being on the playground, he noticed that the noises were different. He could hear cicadas and birds mingling with the laughter of his peers. After school, he often dragged himself home famished. The truth could not be hidden from his older sister despite all his efforts.

'Are you hungry, Arif'? Would you like me to make you something?' Arif pretended not to hear.

Apa persisted. 'I can tell when you're hungry because you don't answer me. I can make some puffed rice with peppers and onions and a little sugar if you like,' she would offer.

Arif politely nodded when offered food, knowing how ashamed his sister would feel when he was constantly hungry.

Apa could not feed her family when the cupboards were bare and puffed rice was unavailable, resulting in an uneasy silence until dinner.

On evenings when he returned home hungry Arif would volunteer to care for Joy. For dinner, Apa had already fried *rotis*. 'Apa, could I take Joy for a walk?' he asked. 'I feel like some fresh air.'

'Oh please, Arif. That would be great,' Apa replied. 'He is really clingy today. Maybe some fresh air will do him good. Be sure to grab his milk bottle from the meat safe,' she called from the kitchen. 'He'll take it from your hands and feed himself if he's hungry. And make sure you are back for dinner.'

Sweating and feeling his heart pound, he imagined how embarrassed he would feel if Apa caught him. Arif ignored the possibility that she might find out. It wasn't in her character to misplace one grain of rice.

After taking the baby bottle from the meat safe, Arif grabbed two *rotis* from the bench plate and slipped them into his pocket. He carried his nephew down the street towards the river, where they walked along a narrow path through trees and scrub. Few people were around.

Arif sang a little marching song in baby talk. He looked into Joy's eyes and smiled. When they reached the shade, Arif paused and looked down at the dirt, enjoying the brisk pace of his stride. He pulled pieces of *roti* from his pocket making sure to keep a careful hold on to the baby. This secret ritual, his meal of shame, consumed him completely. He spat out the bread into the dirt as he chewed it. His mouth was filled with sand.

He took another flat bread from his pocket and this also was hopelessly covered in fine white sand. What could possibly have caused this? It must have come from his participation in the long jump while at school. Joy stopped gurgling and placed a hand on his cheek as hot tears dripped down his face. If he had another pair of shorts, he would have changed after school, but he only had two pairs; when he wore one pair, the other was either soaking in soapy water or hanging from the clothes line to dry.

Arif would see his Apa whenever he visited the country now. He was loved a lot by Apa. When he visited Apa, he still remembered stealing roti from her meat-safe as a child. Shame gripped him. Sometimes he felt compelled to tell Apa about roti-stealing. If he told Apa about the incidents, he thought he might be able to get rid of the felony that had plagued him since childhood! Yet, he thought Apa should have felt more ashamed and disheartened had he told her what he had done. Arif could not do that. Apa was so dear to him.

While living with Apa, Bhai, and his niece and nephew Arif learned not to talk to people he didn't know. The elderly people in the village tended to ask children their father's name and Arif' knew this would lead to questions such as, 'Where do you live? What happened to your dad?' and so on.

Such probing brought him close to tears and close to trembling in anger. He was unsure if these emotions were directed at his parents or God and felt guilty for thinking such thoughts.

One day, Arif accompanied Bhai to the local market where

Bhai chatted with the market stallholders, choosing all the best produce that he could afford. The rohu fish went into one bag and the smaller fish into another. A third jute bag was used for vegetables, condiments, oils, sugar, a few kilograms of fine fragmented rice, goat meat and chicken. Arif assumed they were having guests over.

As Bhai still had some business in town, he asked Arif to carry the bags home. Arif readily agreed but soon found they were too heavy to carry in a normal fashion. To prevent them dragging on the ground, he had to sling the handles over his shoulder and keep them suspended with his elbows bent sharply backward. The bags felt heavier and heavier as he walked until he had to stop and slump down under a large tree.

A man, who Arif guessed was in his forties, was also relaxing under the trees and smoking.

'You don't look familiar to me, boy. What's your father's name?' he asked.

Arif was tired. He wanted to avoid any unwanted emotions and so told the man that Bhai was his father.

The man lowered his arms to his side and slowly approached Arif. 'Who are you, boy? Why are you lying to me? I know that man. I work next to him. And I know his son is only one or two years old.'

Arif turned and ran, feeling like his entire body was bouncing with the bags. It was as if someone was pounding him with soccer balls as he ran, his lungs burning, unable to look back for fear of falling.

As he ran past Dak Bungalow, a local government guest

house, he decided he was no longer in danger. He stopped running so he could catch his breath. Many important guests and politicians stayed at Dak Bungalow – a large wooden building – as they travelled across the country.

The man who ran Dak Bungalow was among the most respected and influential people in town and was known as Bungalow Babu. He had two sons. One of them, Ram, was in the same grade as Arif. Despite the fact that Ram lived in a different part of the small town, Arif often asked Apa for permission to visit Ram's place in the afternoons. Even though it would take a long time to walk there and back, Arif didn't mind the long journey.

Arif never entered Ram's house or knocked on the door when he arrived. Instead, he called to him through a window and Ram greeted him from the door. If Ram did not appear, Arif usually found him at the badminton court, playing with his dad and his younger brother, Laxman, whom they called 'Racquet' because he was so dedicated to badminton and played so much of it.

At first, Arif was intimidated by Bangalow Babu but soon found he was friendly and pleasant. Babu used to ask Arif why he didn't bring his badminton racquet. Arif always made excuses about forgetting to bring it. Babu eventually realised the truth and stopped asking. Instead he pointed Arif to the racquets usually reserved for visiting dignitaries..

After Ram had had enough, he and Arif they would take a tennis ball to the section of the long driveway behind the Dak Bangalow and play a game they had invented. Like tennis, the players kicked the tennis ball up into the air so that it bounced once in the boundary of the other player's territory. The concrete driveway was divided into squares and each player would lob the ball back with his foot.

Much concentration and physicality was required but the best part was its lopped rhythm; the sound of the balls bouncing again and again had a compelling swing to it that reminded Arif of his favourite type of percussion.

One day, Arif was so engrossed in the rhythm of the game that he barely cared when it started raining and soon, was really pouring. As rain the poured down his face, blurring his vision, he chased Ram's brightly coloured t-shirt back to the tin carport that served as sheltered parking for Bungalow's guests.

'Wait here,' Ram said and walked towards a door that let guests enter the building from the carport. Arif let himself become entranced by the tropical rain from the safety of the carport. Ram returned a short while later with both his hands under his shirt, looking like a terrible shoplifter.

'What have you got?' Arif asked.

'Look,' said Ram. He pulled his hands out to reveal a small toy car and a big spinning top.

Ram turned a key on the back of the red car, which looked like a Jeep with an open top. He placed it on the ground and let it go. Ram was obsessed with red. With a high-pitched roar like that of the motorbikes that tore through town, the car surged forward. It followed a surprisingly straight trajectory through the long carport, out past the guests' luxury cars, and in danger of getting wet if it left the shelter of the carport.

Ram, pointed towards the car. 'Go, Arif,' he yelled.

With a leap, Arif managed to stop the car when it was a metre away from making an exit. He placed his foot on the edge of a giant puddle to stop it. With a swiping motion, he picked it up and gently returned it to Ram, cradling it in his hands like a delicate baby chick.

'Thank you,' said Ram and turned his attention to the spinning top. He placed it on the ground and coaxed the strap through its base. As he let go, he spun it rapidly using an outstretched fingertip to steady it as he pulled hard on the strap. As it spun, it sounded like the crackling of a campfire. Its red and yellow paint blurred into each other. The boys bent down, their faces ever closer, light dancing off their cheeks, their eyes wide in fascination. Arif felt a sense of pride for his friend's fortune.

4

In the spring before Arif entered Grade 6, his mother asked him to return home to the family's modest house where life had become more stable after his father's death. His older brother, Bhaijan, was in his last year of university and about to enter the workforce, and his second oldest sister, Dina, was now married and had moved out of the family home.

During one of Dina's visits, Arif was playing with his younger siblings in the front yard while his mother combed coconut oil through Dina's hair as they conversed in hushed tones.

Although the children were chasing butterflies with sticks, Arif doubted they would harm anyone. But he was careful not to let them wander too far.

Arif thought his sister sounded distressed. He stepped closer to the house, trying to conceal his skinny body behind a papaya tree's slender frame while still keeping an eye on the three younger children as they darted back and forth. The children continued trying to knock the butterflies out of the air, but the butterflies seemed safe.

'It was horrible, Maa, I couldn't believe it,' he heard Dina moan as he tuned into the conversation inside the house. 'Your son-in-law ripped the bedsheet off me in the middle of the night and started shouting at me, calling me a beggar.'

Maa caressed her forehead as she combed the coconut oil through her daughter's thick, long hair. Her voice trembled, 'My poor darling, I am so sorry. I wish it weren't this way.'

Arif could only imagine the embarrassment his mother still felt that she had nothing to offer the couple or the groom's family for the wedding, No gifts, no money, no dowry. Nothing. His sister sobbed.

Dina continued, 'The other day, he came home for lunch and I brought him food to the table. I made curry, rice and pickles, and served him lunch on a nice plate then went to serve myself. As I was holding my plate, he shook my hand and threw rice everywhere. He told me to eat off the floor as I didn't own any plates. I ate what he left after he went back to work.

Maa still seated behind his sister, listened intently while she tenderly combed. Arif saw she was crying, her sobs in sync with his sister's.

Arif fumed at his brother-in-law's behaviour. He felt powerless. How he wished he could confront him, and with calm, but powerful words, make him see the error of his ways. Arif would be a hero. But he knew that wasn't going to happen. He never got angry at people in person, although he could get very huffy, and often with little provocation. Maa joked that he was 'born huffy'. Maybe, but he knew his huffiness would not help in this situation and he dismissed any thoughts of confrontation.

During his time at university Arif maintained good relationships with his fellow students yet never felt the need to join them when they gathered on the green lawn between the boys' and girls' dormitories after classes had ended for the day. Instead, he would return to his hostel, wash his face and fix himself a snack before going for a walk along the river.

His close friends were his next door neighbours, Azahar and Sayeed, who lived on the third floor. At least one of them would accompany him every evening as he walked through the cool shady vegetation along the riverbank or along the railway tracks where the harsh afternoon sun shone directly into their eyes.

Along the riverbank, there were no straight lines, confusing one's perception of distance. It was a damp, cool, intimate space. You could only see as far as the trees and shrubs directly in front of you allowed. The railway tracks, in contrast, seemed to shoot straight into infinity with the two rails seeming to converge until they touched, right on the horizon.

Three ancient silk-cotton trees offered the boys daytime respite from the cruel light and heat at a favourite spot along the tracks. With his elbows propped up on his knees, tired from his day of classes, Arif often sat in the shade, nursing his head with his hands, while his friends chatted and joked, snapping sticks and throwing rocks. When ants and other insects went about their business, he stared at the ground, tracking them through patches of grass and lichens as they passed. From above, what looked like a broken green fuzz was a complex little ecosystem, full of novelty and diversity. This miniature world consumed his mind. Often he stared into the distance, lost in the anonymity of vast distances and giant spaces. At other times he stared towards the point where the tracks touched the horizon.

Whenever Arif sat under those silk-cotton trees, he always worried about something. His world was uncertain; he sensed he lacked something. Everything he did felt insecure as if it could suddenly disappear. This included his stationery, uniform, lunch and tuition fees.

These spiralling rumination sessions filled his head with memories that were replayed over and over. A warm night and insects were the first things to come to mind when the sun set. Memories of his mother singing soft, lilting lullabies to his three youngest siblings in the next room in a voice as sweet as honey. The aroma of her delicious food lingered in the air.

When Arif was a child he heard old songs drifting in the door of his shared bedroom when he sat with his older siblings doing homework. It was a casual atmosphere. Maybe one was spread across the floor, surrounded by papers and pens. Others studied on their beds. The one small reading desk was mainly reserved for those working on geometry or sketching projects, otherwise there were arguments about who should use it.

There was always a feeling of compounded boredom. Arif wished he could be in one of the other sons, lying on Maa's warm lap, listening to stories and lullabies. But he knew that was not possible; she needed to take care of the younger children and he had already had his turn. Things were always simpler and happier during Eid, the religious festival marking the end of Ramadan and the end of fasting. Maa was always more relaxed then. She would wait for Arif and his siblings as they returned from prayers, wearing her brightest, newest saree, her skin still feeling cool after her bath. When Arif approached with a slight bow of his head, she placed her hands either side of his head and pull him into her chest.

In the midst of the soothing and relaxing sound of Maa's heartbeat, other sounds faded away. Maa's hands tightened their embrace and as he became enmeshed in her saree, he felt himself slipping into sleep. She would step back and kiss his cheeks and, as the cooling, cucumber-like scent of her face cream filled his nostrils, he felt reborn.

'May God bless my little angel and give him a long, healthy life,' she said, holding him close to her heart.

After his father died, these family feasts became increasingly important to him. He still felt his father's presence at the table, even though he had only sparse memories of the man's life. His older siblings at times seemed thoughtful and distant, while the younger ones had no memory of their father at all.

There was one special moment that Arif would never forget. His father, referred to by his children as Baba, had returned from work that evening. He was greeted by the children and Maa smiled softly as she handed him a yellow envelope. A curious smirk crossed Baba's face. As he carefully removed the letter from the envelope as he raised an eyebrow quizzically.

He looked down at Arif with a smile on his face. He patted his Arif's head and rubbed his shoulders.

'My little Arif is a genius,' he proclaimed. 'Well done, my son.' He leaned down to give him a kiss on the cheek. 'He will be a great scientist. The Newton of the village,' his father continued.

In his fourth year at university, Sayeed started seeing a girl called Rita, a first-year student in the chemistry department with Arif. Arif got along well with Rita. She had an effortless charm and was extremely clever, with empathy and a natural curiosity in others.

Rita lived in the women's hostel and ate her meals in the cafeteria with her friends. Occasionally, Rita prepared a feast for herself and her friends in the hostel kitchen and on the way to meet her girlfriends in the park, dropped some off at Sayeed's room. She always sent extra as she knew that Sayeed and his friends were inseparable, especially on feast night.

Rita was an amazing cook. She sent the boys parcels of delicious chicken curries with plenty of green chillies, or catfish curries with green bananas and even more green chillies. She was always incredibly generous. A typical Rita package contained her delicious *bhuna khichuri*, cooked with just enough rice to separate the grains from each other, and with just enough lentils to pop out. Often, she sent her *bhuna khichuri* with lamb liver stew as a change from the food they ate from the cafeteria, which was almost always the same. Dinner consisted of a small bowl of curry with one piece of goat meat and two pieces of potato; a very thin dhal, in which no lentils could be detected, and a bowl of rice. Rita's food seemed like a royal banquet in comparison.

Rita even organised picnics for Sayeed and his friends. She prepared the entire meal and probably would have paddled everything across the river had the boys not insisted on doing it. The picnic spot was on the opposite riverbank from the university, which owned the boats, and it was an easy paddle when the river was low.

Giant water grasses called *kashbon* lined the riverbanks. They were famed for their elegance and giant wispy white flower spikes, which caught the wind in majestic ways. They reached skywards and always seemed to be moving.

Arif was always glad to be amongst the *kashbon*. The soothing sound of wind through the flower spikes was one of the most beautiful expressions of the wind he had experienced. Little wonder it was celebrated by poets and musicians.

After mooring the boat to the jetty, they disembarked, usually with hilarious clumsiness, and found a comfortable spot. Sayeed handed Arif and Azahar the picnic blanket.

'Here, put this down, but make sure you spread it nicely. No creases.'

To Arif he sounded stressed and slightly condescending. Arif imagined it was hard for Sayeed to keep up with Rita's knack for perfection. 'It would be easier to do what he asked if he wasn't grinning like an idiot all the time,' Azahar said, himself grinning like an idiot.

Once the blanket was perfectly level, Rita started laying out the food. First, she placed a tiffin carrier in the middle of the blanket and placed four small bowls and glasses around it. Then she laid out condiments in the spaces between the bowls and the tiffin, keeping to a mandala-like geometry that Arif enjoyed.

She placed a bowl of green chillies, a bottle of ketchup, one or two chutneys and a small salt shaker around the mat and then opened the tiffin. The aromas of her dishes burst out, giving a preview of the delicious tastes to come as she laid them out, keeping her perfect geometry.

After everyone was satisfied and the picnic utensils were packed away, Arif and Azahar walked upstream, leaving the lovers to themselves. They sat on the jetty, watching their boat bobbing on the river while listening to the babble of the water birds and the seductive rattle of the *kashbon* in the breeze. Arif listened in fascination when Azahar sang old romantic songs in a low quiet voice.

Azahar had a beautiful singing voice perfectly matched to the mood of the old songs and the sounds of moving water and the rattling *kashbons* created the illusion of distant percussion. Even if the lovers were too far from them to hear Azahar's singing, Arif was sure that it helped with the atmosphere in some way. Sometimes he turned to sneak a peek at his friends, whose silhouettes seemed merged in romantic talk and touch, but he soon looked away in embarrassment.

Instead, he turned his gaze back towards the river and closed his eyes. How he wanted a dreamy, affectionate and intelligent woman in his life. He had so much to share, so much love, accumulated pain, and untold huff to express.

5

On their afternoon walks down by the river, Arif always suggested that they stroll through the lecturers' residential area. The reason was Arif's worst kept secret about himself. Both his friends knew the only reason he wanted to take that path was so he might catch a glimpse of a girl named Ruba.

Ruba was the daughter of one of the lecturers and, although she was also a student at the university, she lived with her family in the teachers' area. Occasionally she and Arif caught each other's eyes on the street. Both smiled politely before Ruba's eyes darted towards the ground.

Arif's eyes usually did the same. But even though he really wanted to speak to her, he never loitered in the area to try to create an encounter; it had to be part of his routine.

Azahar was his family's oldest child. His father, the headmaster of a high school in the countryside, was quietly spoken and polite, despite his intellectual intensity. He was a committed father who visited Azahar every four months or so. He never stayed longer than a couple of nights, and those days never dragged for Azahar or his friends as his father slotted in easily with their group.

Azahar gave his father the bed in his room, and he slept in Arif's room, the pair of them sharing Arif's bed. Arif did not mind this intrusion. How could he when Azahar's mother sent such delicious food? At Azahar's father's request, Arif and Sayeed came to Azahar's room and the four of them ate together while seated on a mat in the middle of the room. Azahar's dad waited until they were all seated and then reached into a bag and pulled out containers of food with a satisfied smirk on his face. He always brought a large bowl of *polao*, with rice so perfect that it was not glutinous in any way. He also brought a big bowl of goat curry plus enough sweets and dessert for all four of them. Azahar's father did the serving and divided the meal equally.

As they ate, Azahar and his father talked about politics and education, but mainly about family. Arif listened intently to these stories. They provided a glimpse of another existence; a life where things were more stable and less tragic.

One typical evening Azahar and Arif walked by the river after class. They were quiet and relaxed, taking long gentle strides along the dirt track.

'I think Shayla is the one for me, Arif,' Azahar said chirpily, seemingly out of nowhere.

Arif thought for a moment. 'Really, Azahar. Why do you think that?'

'I know she comes across as intimidating and tenacious, but she has a very soft heart as well,' Azahar said. 'The sight of beggars in her village leaves her in tears, especially the old women. Her empathy is strong. Maybe too strong.'

'She is certainly tenacious,' said Arif. 'Not many girls around here go running or climbing trees, and even fewer fish and swim in the river. I've heard she's even threatened to punch boys who don't play fair. Doesn't her fieriness scare you a bit? Aren't you afraid she's going to whack you?'

'That is exactly what I fear, Arif. She whacks me in the heart every time I see her, and she burns down everything I say when we speak. I swear, she keeps a special madness for me. It's her way of expressing love.'

'That's stupid,' said Arif. 'You sound idiotic when you babble about things you know nothing about. When did you become Azahar, the Great Love Guru?'

'Don't mock me. Did I say something to make you angry?' asked Azahar.

'Nothing at all,' said Arif. 'I just need to study, and I don't want to spend my time talking about rubbish.'

'Your joyless routine is strangling your life, Arif.' said Azahar, passionately. 'Every night you return to your room early, go to sleep early and wake up early. Eventually you'll find that your life drones on and on and ...'

'I've heard enough Azahar. Thanks for your observations. I don't want to hear anymore. Goodnight,' said Arif, departing in a huff.

'Goodnight, Arif,' said Azahar, who remained standing

motionless on the pathway.

Arif walked back to the hostel with the sun beginning to set as he passed through the teachers' quarters. Sayeed hadn't come that night. He was probably with Rita, deep in conversation or maybe in an embrace. What if Azahar got serious with Shayla and he stopped coming too?

Arif glanced around the courtyard hoping to see Ruba. If only she was around, tonight was the night he would muster the courage to speak to her. The annoyance he had felt towards Azahar had fed his resolve to not end up alone in the evening.

There was no sign of Ruba. Few people were about, apart from two men smoking cigarettes next to a staircase. A tan coloured, short-haired dog sniffed around some garbage bins. Otherwise, Arif was essentially alone.

He started daydreaming and was transported to the other side of the riverbank, where he was holding Ruba's hand. They were walking barefoot on the soft white sand. All around them clumps of *kashbon* swayed in the breeze.

'How long have we been walking? I've lost all sense of time,' Ruba asked.

Arif looked back at where they had just walked and smiled.

'I have no idea, Ruba,' he finally said. 'It could be a hundred years; it could be fifteen minutes. I don't know.'

'Oh Arif, we've come so far and it's getting dark. I need to get home before sunset or I'm sure to get a smack,' she said.

'A smack?' Arif imagined himself saying, slightly huffily. 'Who would smack you?'

'Who else can but my mother?' Ruba replied.

'Your mother still smacks you?' Arif asked.

'Smack me or pull my hair. I am not allowed to make any noise, or I get even more punishment. She doesn't want disgrace in front of the other lodgers.'

'Maybe I should come with you. If you introduce me to her, I can explain that we simply walked too far and we meant no harm. If she still comes to beat you, I'll block her off with my back and she can beat that until she exhausts herself.'

Arif gave a smile and a movie-star tilt of his eyebrow.

'What a hero my man is,' Ruba said as she pressed herself into his arms and they kissed intensely.

But none of that would happen tonight. Arif was almost at his dorm and the sun had gone down on his hopes of seeing Ruba that evening.

The next night, after a long day of classes, Arif and Azahar walked through the teachers' quarters on the way to the riverbank. Arif felt a mix of anxiety and excitement that he was barely able to hide from his face as they walked past Ruba's house.

Azahar drew an apprehensive, deep breath. 'Why don't you try talking to Ruba instead of carrying all this tension? She's a nice girl. I don't think she'll bite you, and you don't have to tell her that you like her. Say anything. Even silly things can win a girl's heart. Girls love to laugh.'

Arif glanced back at Ruba's house and felt he was a safe enough distance away to talk freely. He gave nervous laugh.

'Of course I'm not going to walk up and share my feelings uninvited. If she doesn't feel the same way it would turn into a very short, very awkward conversation. But I can't go falling in love at the moment. It will only cause a scandal especially if my grades start to suffer. My maa, my bhai, they would be shocked. When I give someone my love, I want it to be free and unleashed. But right now, it's shackled, and it needs to be. Too many sacrifices have been made so I can get to this point.'

The two friends went silent. Arif stared along the track that led to the riverbank up ahead. It was like a deep, dark portal in a chaotic green morass.

The two boys had followed the river to the point where it met the railway tracks. Now they sat down under a tree. Azahar picked up a stone and threw it at an old stump across the tracks. The rock hit the stump and somehow ricocheted back, hitting the railway track with a loud *ping*.

'Good shot,' said Arif, as Azahar raised a clenched fist in celebration.

Azahar looked at his friend compassionately and placed a hand on his shoulder. He turned his attention away as the railway lines started to vibrate, steadily increasing in volume. His face grew excited.

'What is it, Azahar?' asked Arif.

'Do you have a ten-penny coin? Quick, Arif,' shouted Azahar.

Arif fumbled through his pockets. 'Maybe. Why are you shouting? Why do you want a ten-penny coin?'

Azahar grew steadily more excited, waving his hands around. 'All I have are some quarter-penny coins. I'd rather put tin on the track than brass. I will give you a ten-penny back. Come on Arif.'

'But why?' Arif displayed a ten-penny piece in the palm of his hand.

Azahar snatched the coin and scrambled over the gravel embankment. He placed the coin on the nearest rail as a train loomed in the distance. He stepped back across the gravel and their eyes widened with excitement as the flickering shadow of the train sped straight past them. The train only had three carriages but there were enough passengers on the roof and hanging on to the sides to fill another three carriages. There was a stuttering metallic cacophony as the engine clanged past, and its wheels clipped the rails. Yelled conversations came blasting out through the open windows. The noise suddenly faded. Moments later only the smell of hot metal and cigarette smoke remained.

Azahar pointed to the track where the coin had been. Arif looked down and saw in its place a long, flat, sliver of tin. It was almost perfectly polished. As Arif stepped forward with a smiling face, he saw his distorted reflection in it. And then Azahar's as his friend moved to his side.

6

rif stood in the shower with his eyes closed, his mind on water and its many quirks and traits.

'*What an amazing molecule,*' he thought. '*Its covalent nature means it can express itself as a solid, a liquid or a gas. On top of that it is the ultimate solvent and therefore the building block of all life.*'

He kept marvelling until he acknowledged his procrastination, and stepped out of the shower on a cold, bleak winter morning.

After getting dressed in his most mature shirt, Arif entered the kitchen where Nira greeted him with a cup of tea.

'Thank you, Nira,' he said and took a cautious sip. 'Your timing is amazing as always. This tea is the perfect temperature.'

Since he had stopped taking milk Arif had learnt to be more careful when drinking his tea to avoid scalding his mouth.

Nira smiled. The kitchen smelled delicious that morning and breakfast was already on the table. Arif was to realise that instead of his usual soft-boiled egg Nira had fixed him an omelette. Omelettes were usually a weekend food.

Nira always served her omelettes with lots of thinly sliced onions and green chillies and although the onions and chillies were plentiful the omelette looked different this morning, it seemed more pale than usual. Arif broke some off with his fork and put it in his mouth. He tasted it for a few moments.

'Nira, this omelette seems a bit funny. It's so pale and it tastes different as well,' said Arif. 'I mean, it's nice. But it's different. Like it's missing something.'

'There are only egg whites in that omelette. There's no yolk. What do you think?' asked Nira.

'No yolk?' said Arif, befuddled. 'That's it; we're not buying those eggs again.'

Nira smiled. 'It's not the eggs, Arif. It was me, I took the yolk out for you, they are full of cholesterol. You can have yolks on the weekend.'

'I don't have a problem with cholesterol, Nira. My readings are fine.'

'High cholesterol diets are bad for you. The foods you eat now can harm you in the long run,' said Nira.

'First sugar and milk were taken out of my tea. Next the yolk in my omelette disappears. What next? Omelettes that are just an eggshell for me to crunch on? A cup of hot water?' Arif shook his head and smiled. 'Maybe, if you want me to eat such strange food, you should serve *parathas* too. *Parathas* make any meal go down.'

Parathas were pan fried flat bread that Nira usually saved for weekends. Arif always had *parathas* with his omelette on the weekend and it was one of his favourite meals.

'Sorry honey, no *parathas* … are you annoyed with me?'

'No,' Arif exclaimed. 'I'm having fun observing your strange behaviour. But I do fear that my diet is rapidly shrinking, that one day I will wake up and there'll be nothing that I can eat at all. Sugar's not a problem. Cholesterol's not a problem. Why can't I eat everything?' asked Arif, tucking into his omelette.

'Arif, those are the words of a proud and foolish man. When you continue to eat unhealthy foods, how long will God protect you?

Arif smiled. 'I think you're right, Nira. Can you tell me what other foods will soon disappear from my diet?'

'There is nothing to worry about. You can eat more salad at lunch and less rice at dinner, but any change will be barely noticeable. Are you sure I didn't bother you?'

Arif continued smiling as Nira sat next to him with a cup of tea in her hands. 'Nira you haven't annoyed me at all. I never knew anyone could care so much. I love your spark, I enjoy seeing it, I love it so much.'

Nira looked down as her cheeks took on a slight blush.

'I wish I didn't have to work today so we could go for a picnic,' said Arif. 'We could take *parathas*, hot chicken *bhuna*, sweets, lots of sweets and we could take a boat across the river where the *kashbon* grows and do nothing but eat and talk all day. We wouldn't return until it was dark.'

'But how would we get back in the dark?' asked Nira.

'We would have candles, my dear … and I'd steer the boat by the light coming from the other side of the bank. Anyway, we could stay in a small village like the ones that we grew up in. The streets would be so quiet that we would have them all to ourselves. You would suddenly start running and I'd chase you and perhaps you would fall on to some grass and I would stumble and fall on top of you. And maybe we wouldn't get up for a while,' said Arif with a grin. 'Wouldn't that be fun?'

Nira laughed. 'You sound like a boy. A real teenage boy. You're becoming more childish by the day.'

'I can still run pretty fast you know, Nira. I would catch you easily.'

'You would be surprised, Arif. I've still got strong legs and if we did both fall, like in your little story, you would be suffering, but not me. I have had two children. Falling is nothing.'

'I should go,' said Arif. 'I still need to brush my teeth, then I'll come and say goodbye.'

'It's freezing outside. Please make sure to take that new scarf I got you,' she said and pointed in the direction of the front door.

Arif nodded. 'Of course. Thanks, Nira,' he said, and made his final preparations before leaving for work.

Arif stared out his office window at leafless maple trees instead of reviewing his lectures for the following day. Winter had well and truly started and the trees had only a few yellow or red leaves left on each of them.

At any other time of the year, pink and grey feathered galahs would have been making a cacophony in those trees as they fought for maple seeds and perches, but it seemed that they weren't fond of deciduous trees in winter. They had probably retreated to some of the older gum trees that lined the university grounds or had flown north.

Arif heard voices outside. Several students were walking along the road in a loose rabble. They moved in groups of two or three that continually merged and split as conversations and jokes hung in the air. He heard the relief in their voices that classes had ended for the day.

Arif shut down his computer and removed a USB stick. He was done. The students had inspired him. He would review his lectures later. He grabbed a couple of printed journal papers off his desk, placed them in his brown leather satchel and left.

Arif was putting together a lecture on climate change and ocean chemistry, so one of the papers was on ocean acidification and the other was about hypoxia in benthic marine environments. He was proud that it was co-authored by one of his old friends, Hassan. He could not believe that it had almost been two years since the last time they had seen each other.

Every couple of years Arif tried to visit his brothers and sisters in Bangladesh and whenever he was in the country, he dropped in on Hassan. He was now a professor at Dhaka University and the head of the biochemistry department, a fact that filled Arif with great pride.

Although his elder brother, his *bhajan* in the local language, tried to organise a car and sometimes even a driver for him, Arif always rode by rickshaw when he was in Dhaka. He wanted to be thrust straight into the sights, sounds and smells of his old country and to feel every bump on the road.

He loved arriving at the campus and seeing the students,

carefree in the mid-morning sun, out the front of the buildings, in amongst the hawkers and food carts, eating some of his favourite foods such as *chotpoti* and *fuchka*. They all seemed so content, as if the *fuchka* they were clutching represented the happiness of the whole world right there in their fists. If there were two things that energised Arif it was youthful energy and the promise of *fuchka*.

On his last visit, Arif tipped the rickshaw driver and approached an older man who was selling *chotpoti* and *fuchka* from his food rickshaw. 'Brother, can I have a plate of *fuchka* and an extra sprinkle of green chilli on top, please?' he asked the man.

The old man, who had just served a plate of *chotpoti* to a young girl, looked up and smiled at Arif. He seemed genuinely touched. Arif knew that older vendors were usually referred to as 'uncle' at best. He had also seen customers referring to elderly vendors as 'old man', which seemed patronising and disrespectful, so he made a rule of looking out for elderly workers. In university he was known for always choosing the oldest rickshaw driver, much to his friends' amusement.

'Why do you pick the oldest driver? That man looks like he can barely walk?' they asked him, incredulously.

'One day, we'll be old as well, God permitting. This man needs to eat while he is alive. Should I deny him his right to exist because of his age?' Arif answered.

His friends usually cast their gaze downwards and did not mention it again.

The vendor glanced at Arif and handed him a steaming hot plate.

'Here brother, God bless,' he said to Arif, flashing him a gap-toothed smile, already in the process of serving another customer.

Nira would have been upset if she had known Arif was eating *fuchka*, but Arif didn't feel guilty. He felt sorry for Nira. After all, it was Nira who had introduced him to *fuchka* in the first place. These days she was scared to eat street food. She was worried that she might end up being sick and unable to enjoy the rest of the trip. Arif never experienced such problems. He often joked that he could eat fried sheep intestines before bed and wake up hungry for breakfast.

After greeting each other, Hassan suggested that they go and get a meal.

'Have you had lunch yet, Arif? I'm starving,' said Hassan.

'No, not yet. I'm starving too,' said Arif, deciding not to mention the *fuchka* he had just eaten.

Hassan started heading towards the rickshaw drivers next to the gate.

'Hassan, let's walk. I wish to walk the streets and see the sights of my home country and it's not far into town,' said Arif.

'I see that you're still allergic to even the smallest of luxuries, Arif,' grumbled Hassan as he followed Arif away from the rickshaws.

Arif knew that Bangladeshi citizens living in urban areas were embarrassed in the presence of ex-pats such as himself. They tended to avoid some streets at all costs and rushed their guests from one rich area to the next, hoping to avoid any scenes of poverty and squalor. But Arif would have none of that. Travel was a warts-and-all proposition for him, especially in the country of his birth.

'Arif are you and your family busy on Friday?' asked Hassan. 'Jesmine has invited you all to dinner at our house. You, Nira and the girls.'

'Thank you, Hassan. Maybe you should contact Nira directly and ask her,' said Arif. 'I forget everything when my brain goes into holiday mode and I am away from work.'

'Okay, I'll tell Jesmine to contact Nira. It will just be a normal meal, not a banquet or anything. Just a modern, informal meal with nothing too fancy.'

Arif laughed.

'What's so funny, Arif?'

'Forgive me, Hassan. It's just that every time we come back here we're told we'll be served normal food, like we've become so westernised that we can't enjoy the food we grew up with.'.

'No, we really will be eating plain food,' said Hassan. Things have changed here as well. People avoid eating rich foods at home now. Besides, we need to start thinking about our health. We don't have the iron-clad metabolisms that we once had.'

'Does everything have to be age related?' Arif asked. 'As long as you're eating delicious food, what does it matter what your age is?'

'Arif, you sound so simplistic. You are a professor of chemistry. You understand that a person's physiology and chemical processes change as we age,' Hassan reminded him.

'But would you really feed us nothing but rice and vegetables?'

'I'm not cooking. I am not sure what will be served. But we

have made it a habit of not eating rich food at home,' said Hassan.

'Ah, but do you eat rich foods when invited into other people's homes?' asked Arif with a broad smile.

Arif and Hassan walked past a street vendor who was making *pithas*, steaming four of the delicious cakes at a time while mixing rice flour, coconut, jaggery and milk in a large bowl. Arif stopped and watched the woman practice her craft. These were the moments he could not get anywhere else. He turned to Hassan.

'Can I buy you some *pithas*, Hassan? You're not at home and these look delicious,' he said.

Hassan grabbed Arif's hand and spun his body around so they were facing each other. Arif stared at him, mouth agape.

'Have you gone mad? We are not far from the university, there are students all around us. And you want me to stand here on the footpath eating *pithas* off a plastic plate?' Hassan muttered sternly.

'Don't teachers eat *pithas* around here?' asked Arif sarcastically.

'Of course they eat *pithas* but not on the footpath. Look, I know a nice restaurant that makes all the traditional food, perfect for people like you who are coming home and desire the meals that they grew up with. They even make delicious *pithas*. But please, let us find a rickshaw and get off the street. I'll buy lunch,' offered Hassan.

When Arif realised he was still daydreaming in his office, he grabbed his things and promptly left the building. He took a deep breath of fresh air and approached his car, reaching into his pocket to press the button on his keyring. The sound of the car's doors opening brought him a strange satisfaction, like the sound of a pet cat purring in response to being patted.

The car was three years old, but it looked brand new to Arif. There were no scratches and hardly any dust or dirt on its shiny black paint job. Nira had picked the colour and the model, but it was Arif who was obsessive about its upkeep.

The car pulled out of the university driveway and on to the main road in time to beat the main rush of traffic. This meant it would only take him half an hour to get home. He relaxed into the drive and into the rhythm of the pre-peak traffic, but instead of taking his usual route, he detoured into a side street and pulled up next to the back door of the massage parlour.

He entered the shop, triggering a cacophony of chimes The aroma of massage oil and incense assaulted his senses. Incense smoke whooshed around him as he stepped further inside.

Footsteps could be heard in another room and then the door opened behind the reception desk, momentarily illuminating the room. The door closed again and Arif squinted through his glasses.

'Er... hello?' he said. For a terse moment, he heard no response.

'You've come back? I really didn't think I'd see you again,' a woman's voice replied. It was Amelia.

'I remembered that last time I was here I forgot to give you a tip,' Arif exclaimed.

'That's not important,' Amelia said. 'You didn't enjoy the massage, so you didn't tip; that's understandable. Besides, no one in Australia tips apart from drunk, old, rich guys who want to show off.'

'Well, I want to tip you and I am neither drunk nor particularly rich,' said Arif with a smile.

'I can't take your money unless I offer some service,' said Amelia. 'Would you like to try another massage?' she joked.

Arif thought for a moment. 'Hmmm, maybe just my neck and my shoulders,' he finally said.

Amelia laughed gently.

'I'm not taking anything off tonight,' he added. 'Not my jumper, not my shirt, not my singlet … nothing.'

Amelia continued to laugh with a hand over her mouth as Arif reached into his pocket and pulled out his wallet. He removed two fifty-dollar notes and offered them to her. She hit a button on the cash register and stashed the money inside. She pointed towards the curtain that led to the studios.

'Wait over there and I'll be through in a minute,' she said.

Arif looked around the reception area casually, hoping he would notice some overlooked detail that would help explain the place, but he saw nothing new apart from a security camera above the door.

'Please come through,' Amelia said, as she stood behind the beads in the corridor that led to the massage studios.

Arif followed her into the corridor and then into one of the studios.

'I'll be right back,' she said.

Arif sat on the bed. This room seemed dingier than the last time he was here. The low-power light globe gave off a greyish glow that barely made it to the corners off the room. Even so, the linen he was sitting on seemed clean and fresh, and even as if it had been ironed. There was barely a crease apart from the corners. The only other things on the bed were a pillow with a white cover topped by a blue towel.

Amelia returned to the room with a small basin full of steaming water. White towels were draped over her forearms. She now wore an apron over her clothes and Arif thought she looked like a nurse. She approached the bed where Arif was sitting, leaving behind a plume of aromatic steam, and placed the bowl on a small table beside the bed.

'Please take off your shoes and lie on the bed,' she said, pointing towards the pillow. Arif took off his glasses and placed them on the table then ground his head into the pillow until his neck felt comfortable.

Amelia had never had a customer as confusing as Arif . Generally, if people did not like a massage, they would not return, but this guy did. She could not figure it out. She had customers who would fall asleep during massages, some of them snoring so loud that she was afraid her boss would tell her off. Others would only pretend to be asleep, so they had an excuse for groping her. Others pretended to scratch their noses as she was bending down to apply pressure to their foreheads so they could brush against her chest. Arif did not strike her as one of those creepy guys, but she couldn't work out his intentions.

When she first started working at the parlour, the owner of the business, Ms Maliwan, spent a lot of time training her and had warned her early on that many of her customers would be quite unpleasant. There would be some nice customers as well, but sometimes people who were perfectly nice in normal life would behave badly in the secret world of the massage parlour. Their anonymity could bring out their worst tendencies and then after the massage, they would get dressed and become respectable family men all over again.

Ms Maliwan told all the girls that if they pleased their clients, they could make hundreds of dollars a night on tips alone and although penetrative sex was illegal in the parlour, the smart girls knew how to please their clientele in other ways.

For the first few days of her training, Amelia blushed and looked down whenever Ms Maliwan mentioned sex and she realised that Ms Maliwan had noticed this disapprovingly.

Amelia was unhappy that the shop took sixty per cent of what clients paid and that there were no specific breaks given; the girls were expected to eat between clients. But she would never mention such opinions to Ms Maliwan.

Ms Maliwan was a stoney-faced woman who spoke four languages and was obviously a veteran of the massage industry. She was connected to a network of migration agents whose job it was to find girls like Amelia to staff her businesses. Many girls were contracted to stay at the parlours for two to three years before they could move on.

Amelia was not sure if any of her fellow students at the language school were also in her situation, but she felt it was almost inevitable. The school she went too seemed expensive and exploitive. She had to keep reminding herself that she would not be there long. As soon as she finished her one-year language course, Amelia planned on doing a two-year post-graduate diploma in business communication while she waited for her employment contract to run out.

On her first official day, Amelia felt a headache brewing and secretly hoped that no customers would come in for her shift, even if it meant going home poorer than when she left that morning.

She waited behind the reception desk, trying to do an English crossword, but could not concentrate as she kept glancing at the front door every few moments. Eventually she heard the chimes and looked up to see the door opening. She felt a lump rise from her stomach and up into her throat. She could hardly breathe.

A tall, slender looking man stepped into the store and looked around the reception area before fixing his gaze on Amelia. He seemed to be in his mid to late thirties, with short, messy hair. He wore a black singlet with racing cars on it and a pair of green khaki cargo shorts. His biceps were covered in red and black tattoos underneath fuzzy blond body hair. His legs were the same and Amelia cringed at the thought of touching them. He didn't smile or say anything as he approached the counter.

'Hi,' she said. 'Can I help you?'

'Just an hour,' said the man. He stared at Amelia's chest with emotionless greyish-blue eyes.

'Okay,' answered Amelia, trying to hide her nerves. 'That will be $75, please.'

The man reached into his pocket and grabbed an old, bloated leather wallet that looked like it was falling apart. He handed her a card and Amelia could see that his hands were covered in black grime, like he had just come from work.

'I'm sorry,' said Amelia. 'We can only take cash, sir.'

'Fucking bullshit,' said the man, clearly unimpressed as he continued staring at her chest.

'You're all scamming, dodgy cunts,' he whined. He dropped two fifty-dollar notes behind the desk with a dismissive flick of the wrist.

Amelia bent down to pick up the notes, happy to look away from the man and his leering, dehumanising stare. She put the notes in the till before handing the man his change.

'Please wait here,' Amelia instructed him and went through the door behind the reception desk.

She reappeared a few moments later, parting a pair of white curtains that led to the corridor where the massage studios were. There were two studios on each side of the corridor. She led the man into one of them and pointed to a white robe on a coat hanger.

'Take off your clothes and put on this robe,' she instructed. 'I'll be back in a moment.'

Amelia turned and walked out of the room, leaving the man as he jostled with his belt, swearing under his breath. She walked into the staffroom at the end of the corridor, took a basin from under the sink, and filled it with hot water from the tap. Next, she used a large eye dropper to add scented oils from a brown glass bottle. As she added the oils to the steaming water, tears welled in her eyes.

'It's just the oils and the steam,' she told herself, trying to steady her shaking hands.

She had been so excited when she first signed up for a package with an agent promising her a job and a place at a prestigious language school in Australia. It sounded too good to be true and deep down Amelia knew that it probably was. But it was the only option she could afford, and even then it was a significant amount of money for her.

Her parents were not rich and although she had never gone hungry, they could only contribute a small amount of money. And they approved of her making the most of her mathematics degree by learning an international language, even if they did not know the finer details of the journey.

She knew the move would be challenging, but she was also determined.

Amelia gazed into the steamed-up mirror above the sink and stared into her own eyes for a split second before she tore herself away and returned to the studio. The customer was lying on the bed with the robe on back to front, so the opening was on his front side. He had removed all his clothes, even his underwear, and was grinning at Amelia as he lay on his side with his legs dangling.

Amelia froze on the spot. She instantly hated that grin. She imagined tipping the tub of hot water all over him and running away. Taking a deep gulp, she stepped closer to the massage table and placed the basin and some white towels on the small bench next to it. The man glanced down his body and Amelia felt sick.

'Sir, please lie on the table properly and roll over,' she instructed, her voice trembling.

The man glared at her for a moment then smiled as he rolled over on to his chest. Amelia almost gagged at the sweaty and musty air that wafted off the massage table, displaced by the wallop of his belly.

The sight of the hairy behind was confronting. It disturbed her. She grabbed one of the warm towels and looking away as she placed it over the offending orifice. The man responded by exhaling loudly and then let out a series of horrifying burps that filled the room with the stench of sour beer. Amelia could hardly breathe. She thought the smell of the oils was bad, but stale beer and whatever else was even worse.

Ms Maliwan had told the girls always to start the massage on the customer's back, neck and shoulders. Customers were less mobile when laying on their bellies so they couldn't grab a girl's hands as easily. It also gave the girls a chance to relax the customers before they turned belly up.

She poured light green herbal oil from a small bottle on to her hands and began massaging the man's shoulders. She worked her way down his back carefully and clinically with the tips of her fingers and her palms. When she made it down to his waist, she resumed back at his shoulders and started the whole process again.

6

'Huh … huh … huh … huh …' The man sounded like an old car idling and his lack of any obvious consciousness enabled Amelia to relax slightly.

She sighed loudly and glanced down, but luckily the man didn't stir so she let herself relax again. A soft smile formed on her face; she was finally going to get some income. She had been relying on savings to pay her rent and that had been eating away at her, mentally and financially. Now she felt hopeful.

She liked her house and she liked her housemates who were from similar backgrounds and were doing similar things in Australia. The migration company had found the house for her and later that evening, she would be going home to her flat with her housemate, Ella, who was working the same shift. As Amelia worked her way down the man's arms with a series of gentle squeezes, she remembered the advice Ella had given her earlier in the day.

'Melbourne's expensive,' she had told her. 'You won't survive in Melbourne doing only body massages, especially when the parlour takes sixty per cent.'

Ella had been giving here clients 'happy endings' since she started.

Ella had arrived in Australia as a student two years earlier. Her migration agent had enrolled her in an English language course, which she completed in six months. She next enrolled in a one-year Certificate IV in English course which she successfully completed. Her agent then enrolled her for a two-year advanced diploma in business management, certain that she would stay in Australia for at least two years.

She never attended any school when completing these courses, nor do any assignments on her own. They were all completed for her — and that cost money. And at the end of it all, she was still incapable of writing a single word in English. Even writing *Melbourne* was difficult for her.

As she confided to Amelia, many of her Asian friends were remaining in Australia and obtaining Australian qualifications without any hassles.

'What's the point of standing on the dance floor if you're not going to dance?' she asked Amelia, paraphrasing a saying popular in Thailand. 'The quicker I make my money the quicker I can bring my son over.' She had a young son living with her parents in Taiwan.

As Amelia rubbed the man's wrists with her fingers, she glanced over her shoulder at the clock above the doorway. She had been at it for twenty-five minutes and Ms Maliwan had told her the customer would pay for an hour. But massages could last only for forty-five minutes. The other fifteen minutes were for cleaning up the oils and for the customers to put their clothes back on.

Amelia worked on the man's legs and noticed what skinny little ankles he had. She smiled in surprise that she had found something about him that didn't disgust her. She gave his ankles special attention as she imagined how much stress they must take every day. He snored softly and peacefully. She was sure that he was asleep. There were only ten minutes left.

'Sir ... sir ...,' Amelia purred gently into the man's ear.

'Could you please sit up, sir?' The man's head shook gently. As he turned towards her, his eyes opened groggily. He stared at her in befuddlement.

'Good massage, babe,' he said. 'You put me to sleep.' He laughed. 'Do you have drugs coming out of your fingers or something?'

'No, no drugs,' Amelia said with a broad grin.

'Please sit up so I can properly massage your head and neck. Would you like it soft or rough?' She spoke with a slight purr, exactly as she had been taught.

'Don't tell anyone,' the man, said, 'but I think we'll keep it soft for today.'

He smiled gently and Amelia smiled back. She put more oil on his back and pressed gently against his shoulders and his flanks with her entire forearm. Then she worked up to his neck until she was gently rubbing the base of his skull. His breath became deep and slow and Amelia felt she had complete control over him. He was her puppy and puppet. She finished with a light brush upwards through the hair on the back of his head through to his crown, like she was pulling a silk scarf out of his skull.

'Your massage is finished,' she informed him, with a slight tremble in her voice.

The man stood up in silence.

'I removed all the oil with the hot towels so you can get dressed now. I'll be back in a minute,' she added.

The man stood, still not moving so Amelia shrugged her shoulders and walked out taking the basin and the towels with her.

Back in the small room at the end of the corridor she turned on the water, letting it get hot. She used plenty of soap to lather her hands and arms all the way to her elbows then slowly rinsed it off. Her mind was blank. She returned to the massage room to find her client dressed and smiling.

'Amazing,' he said. 'That was great. Your hands are magic.'

He glanced down at them.

'Well thanks,' she said, bowing her head ever so slightly.

'I'll be asking for you next time I'm here. What's your name?' he asked with a lift of his chin.

'Nicole.'

He reached into his pocket.

'Here, Nicole,' he said as he pulled out his bloated old wallet and removed a fifty-dollar note. 'Take this.'

Amelia was stunned.

'Th-thank you,' she stammered and took the money a little too quickly, as if she feared it might disappear at any moment. She palmed the note and clasped her arms behind her, bowing her head.

'Goodbye,' she said as he left, walking out the door with his back straight.

As she massaged Arif's shoulder Amelia wondered why he had come back. If he had enjoyed the last massage in retrospect, he certainly was not showing any signs of it now. He was as stiff as an old board.

She realised that she did not understand many of her subcontinental customers, or what their motivations were. They were always nervous, as she would observe them on the security camera, pacing around the shop and peeking through the front door glass, as if to make sure that no one had followed them. When one of the ladies entered the reception area to serve them, they seemed to freeze with fear, and panic raged in their eyes.

She found the younger students even stranger, although many were lonely, which she understood well. They were completely shameless in their bargaining so the whole massage seemed like a non-stop bargaining session.

'How much would I have to pay you to take your top off? And your bra?' clients asked.

'How much would it cost to touch your breast?' was the next inevitable question.

Then they would often ask how much it was for a happy ending and if they could pay less if they came quickly.

Amelia had conditioned herself to always agree to happy endings. An extra hundred dollars an hour plus the generous tips that men often gave her after their ejaculation, made it a hard proposition to turn down. Besides, she had to. As far as she knew all the other girls at the shop gave happy endings. She had too as well if she wanted to avoid being blacklisted by certain customers.

Most of the girls would try to initiate happy endings by focussing on the customer's waist, reaching their fingers slightly around to knead the buttocks like bread while trying to brush the back of the testicles with their hands.

Amelia had come a long way since her first happy ending six months ago. She was with Ella that day and business was slow. None of the men who came in showed any interest in her, they all wanted Ella's touch. Amelia tried doing a crossword, but her lack of English made it frustrating and she was alone at reception as a large and imposing man walked through the door. He wore a black, dusty t-shirt matching the black sweaty hair that streaked across his forehead and his red, swollen face.

He looked at her with washed-out, distant blue eyes.

'Oi. Do you do "handies"?' he asked.

Amelia stared at him as she processed what the man was saying. He rolled his eyes and returned to glaring at her.

'Hand job,' he said loudly, as he clenched his fist and jerked off the air in front of him, assuming that she could not understand English.

Amelia's throat went dry. She swallowed hard.

'You need to pay for a massage, sir,' she said, matter-of-factly. '$100 cash up front plus $75 for an hour's massage.'

The man reached for his wallet and pulled out four, fifty-dollar notes.

'Keep the change,' he said. 'And show me the room.'

Amelia led him to a room on the left.

'Please go inside, take off your clothes and put on a robe. I'll be right back,' she instructed.

When she returned with a basin of hot water and perfumed oils, the customer was sitting on the end of the table completely naked. He scanned her body with his cold eyes.

'Lie, down on your stomach please, sir,' she asked him.

'Take off your shirt and bra,' he said, as if it were nothing at all.

Amelia turned her back and slid her hands down her side, taking off her t-shirt in a sensual way, hoping she could waste a few moments touching her own body, which seemed a much nicer proposition. She felt his hand on her shoulder, suddenly whipping her around to face him.

'I'm not here for a striptease,' he said. 'Just take the fucking thing off. I'll give you another fifty.'

Amelia was furious. She wanted to punch the fifty-dollar note down his throat until he choked.

'Thank you,' she said and stripped off her t-shirt like she was about to have a shower in the morning.

'And the fucking bra. Do I have to do it myself?'

The man looked angry and moved to stand up. Amelia quickly reached behind and undid the latch of her bra.

'Good, much better,' he said. 'You've got glorious little tits.'

He breathed heavily as he leered at her with glazed eyes, mouth agape.

He held out his hand and motioned with his fingers for Amelia to get closer, so she stepped towards him. He looked like he was about to pass out at any moment as his erection twitched in the air. As Amelia stared at the man's penis, he grabbed her hand and dragged it down towards it. It felt like a hot iron rod to touch as it quivered in her hands. Amelia crouched between his splayed, hairy legs.

'Go on,' he said. 'It's not gonna rub itself.'

Amelia reached over to the table and picked up a bottle of baby oil, but the man grabbed her wrist.

'Do I look like a baby?' he asked. 'Does my cock look like a baby? No oil. I hate that smell. Use your spit,' he said. Amelia looked at him quizzically.

'Your spit. The stuff that comes out your mouth,' he repeated, forcefully.

Then he opened his mouth and made a gargling sound, as he showed her his tongue covered in saliva. Amelia almost gagged as she sucked saliva into her mouth. When she finally had a mouthful, she pursed her lips as her head hovered above his crotch and she looked down trying to aim the drop of saliva, towards the little red bit, but she missed and it landed in the pubic hair just below his belly. Amelia thought he would get angry but instead he squirmed with pleasure.

'More,' he said. 'Make a fucking mess with that spit.'

Amelia spat and then spat some more, spitting all over the lower regions of this horrible person until the shaft was covered in her saliva. When it was glistening, she started jerking him off.

The man's head fell backwards and his hips tightened and rose towards Amelia as he groaned. Amelia instinctively turned her head the other way but felt bad and fixed her gaze back at what she was doing. His penis seemed to be gulping up the air in front of it.

She remembered once, as a child, when she had travelled with her family through the jungle to visit a festival at a village in the mountains. The village belonged to the Akha people who would feast for four days on local seafood, pork and strong palm wine.

After drinking and eating all day, half-naked women would sing and dance, and the men, who sat around smoking cigars rolled from local plants, would try to sing back, but the cigar smoke and the wine would make their voices seem alien and distant. The main thing Amelia remembered was the killing of the pigs.

A crude iron spike was placed in the fire until red hot at which stage two men grappled a piglet while another man inserted the rod deep into the chest of the animal. For almost half an hour the poor creature bawled and twisted on the pole, until its eyes became dull and it started twitching.

Her customer's body had now become rigid and his toes looked like they were trying to tear themselves off his feet. The man was slanting backwards, breathing through his gaping mouth. The smell of his breath was making Amelia breathless, suffocating for lack of fresh air. His mouth was wide open as he took massive gulps of air. His stinking breath hit Amelia right in the face. The man grunted and moaned with each movement of her hand. His groans increased, becoming louder. A few seconds later it was all over. Suddenly she felt a volcanic eruption of a hot and smelly poisonous lava. The man slumped as he came in her hand. Amelia felt tired and drained.

She had passed another career milestone.

Amelia knew men owned seeds. Men sowed seeds in the field, the fields became full of crops. In the body of the women, with men's seeds, future is born. Amelia looked at her handful of smelly liquid. *This could not be the seeds of men,* she thought, *this is nothing but a mix of blood and pus, the decayed eruption of a man's lustful perverted need.*

Everything surrounding her was becoming dark. She wanted

to vomit. She ran out of the room and reached the washroom in time. She held her hand under running water and threw up into the sink.

Arif was lying stiffly on his back with his eyes closed tight as Amelia worked her way down his arms in a series of squeezing motions. He seemed quiet and distant today as if he were in deep thought. He still didn't seem to be enjoying the massage, as his body was taut, not supple and everything would move as one with every manipulation she tried. Not relaxed at all.

As Amelia leaned over him her chest brushed his. Arif tried to squirm away from her, but he was pinned.

'Are you okay?' Amelia asked.

'Yes, I'm fine.' he said, chirpily. 'I have a slight headache. Nothing serious. But only now I've remembered something I was supposed to do. Can you please finish up, Amelia? I need to go.'

Amelia glanced at the clock on the wall. 'It's only been twenty minutes and you've paid for an hour,' she exclaimed. 'If you go you can't get your money back.'

'I don't want my money back,' he said. 'But I do need to go.'

'Okay, as you like,' she said.

Now it was her turn to glare.

Arif hopped quickly off the table and reached down to get his shoes, distractedly fumbling with the laces and doing a terrible job of putting them on.

Amelia wondered why he didn't concentrate and put them on properly.

She quickly looked away as he stood up straight with his laces done and his hand reaching into his pocket. He removed two, fifty-dollar notes from his wallet and reached out towards her with the money in his hand.

'Please take it,' he said.

Amelia scowled quizzically.

'What's this for?'

'It's nothing, it's just a tip,' said Arif. He waved his hand dismissively.

'Why pay a tip if you're not happy with the massage?' Amelia asked. Her voice sounded full of suspicion.

'If you take the money, I'll be happy,' said Arif,

'Okay. Thank you, Arif,' she said and looked down.

'Can I ask you something?'

Amelia rolled her eyes. She knew she should not have taken the money. There was always a catch. Subcontinental men were often polite and would leave large tips, often for nothing, but soon the requests would start. They would talk about how they were unhappy at home, how they were lonely and alienated and make invitations to visit restaurants and hotels and they would always be gone by ten or eleven o'clock at night.

Arif looked uncomfortable as Ameila stared at him in silence.

'Amelia, I know I may be crossing a boundary here, I even know it's against the rules of the shop, but would you please share your phone number with me? I promise you can trust me.'

This was a common request from subcontinental customers.

They would call on their mobiles before they even got home from the shop and then the phone calls would come at odd hours of the night into the early morning. Amelia stayed silent as Arif reached into his pocket, retrieving a card from his wallet.

'Here is my number, Amelia,' he said. 'You can text me your phone number later if you're comfortable with that.'

Amelia sighed.

'It's not only that it's against the rules of the shop. When I leave here at night, I want to forget all about the job. I don't want customers calling me. But you've been so generous and haven't asked for anything else in return …'

They stood staring at each other for a moment. Arif was the easiest money she could make so she held out her hand and accepted his card. He seemed more confident and determined than before.

'If me taking your card makes you happy then I can accept your tip without feeling any guilt,' she said. 'Good-bye, Arif.'

'Yes. Okay. Great,' mumbled Arif. 'See you, Amelia.'

She parted the curtain and Arif exited into the corridor, smiling, nodding his head, and setting off the chimes as he stepped outside.

7

Arif turned his key in the front door and went straight to the bedroom where Nira was hanging shirts in his wardrobe. Arif froze. Did he still reek of the sickly massage oil?

'You're home early,' Nira said, smiling, before squinting one eye and placing a hand on her hip. 'Are you feeling okay?'

'Yeah, I'm fine, Nira,' said Arif, smiling. 'I couldn't concentrate in the office and I didn't have any more classes, so I came home. The thought of spending time with you was too tempting to stay at work.'

'Stop it,' she laughed, 'You're so insincere sometimes.'

'No, I'm serious Nira,' said Arif. 'Anyway, how was your day off?'

Nira worked for the local government in human services three days a week and had recently turned down a well-paying promotion because it meant she would spend less time with the girls. Arif felt a bit sad that she had put her career on hold, but he loved and respected her instincts as a mother.

'My day's been steady. The girls have been good today,' Nira said.

Arif nodded thoughtfully and tried to shuffle past her and into his wardrobe. But instead of getting past her, Nira stepped towards him, her arms outstretched. She embraced him.

'Arif are you wearing a new cologne?' She screwed up her nose. 'It doesn't smell good, it doesn't suit you at all.'

Arif paused for a moment, as he took a deep breath. Maybe he could tell her that today's class was about the chemistry of essential oil. Or maybe mummification.

Ring-ring. Ring-ring…

Arif exhaled loudly as Nira looked at the phone on her bedside table.

'It must be Maa,' she said. 'Why are you standing there looking stunned, Arif? Do you need help to get changed?' she added sarcastically. She turned towards the phone, allowing Arif to slip into the walk-in wardrobe and fill his nostrils with the smell of clean fabric.

It was a scent that relaxed him. It always reminded him of how his problems disappeared when he was face deep in his mother's saree as a child. In that moment he felt hopelessly out of his depth. Arif had never lied to Nira before… well, not really. He always obfuscated in response to questions like, 'Who's been eating the such-and-such?' or 'Who ate the last such-and-such?' But as a dad, he had the right to embellish the truth in those situations. Was it even a lie when the truth was so obvious?

Arif changed his shirt and his trousers and reached to put the old ones in his laundry basket next to the door. He took some cologne that he used for keeping his clothes fresh from a shelf in front of him and sprayed some inside the laundry basket, making sure that Nira was deep in conversation with her mother and facing away from him.

Nira, who had not uttered a word since saying 'hello', broke her silence. 'Maa, you sent a large parcel only two months ago. You do not need to send any more gifts. We are okay here, Maa, I promise you.'

She paused a moment.

'Hold on, what type of saree was it, Maa?' she asked.

Every few months, a parcel would arrive from Nira's mum and she loved to discuss the different things that she packed into them. She described each item in detail before they were purchased, and then they were reviewed on multiple further occasions.

'Maa, you still don't have a good mobile phone, do you? How about if I bring you a new phone next time I visit?' Nira asked, breaking a long silence.

Nira never sent parcels in return, preferring instead to hoard small items for at least five or six months before any visit back to her mother's place.

There was another pause. 'You could speak to me away from the home phone, and when we talked, we'd be able to see each other. You could see your granddaughters and I can show you around the house and we can compare gardens. You could even give me cooking lessons. Wouldn't it be fantastic?' Nira said.

'Maa, you'll learn. You will be fine. After getting used to it you won't want to use your old phone anymore and I can teach you how to use it in no time.'

Arif enjoyed listening to mother and daughter conversations. It seemed that after girls got married, the relationship between mothers and daughters become more like one between close friends. He eavesdropped a lot as a child and always felt enlightened listening to these discussions.

When his oldest sister married, after his father had died, things were stressful as they had no gifts or dowry to offer, but his mother had told her, 'Wait until your brothers graduate and get good jobs, they will make up for everything. You'll be able to feel proud in front of your husband.'

All his sisters received the same advice and had to accept Maa's hopeful words. Through his eavesdropping, he felt a responsibility towards his sisters and Maa.

Arif grew to hate the way some of his brothers-in-law treated his sisters. The thought of harming those men came easily to him but he knew he did not have the physical strength, so he would have to work hard instead.

'But does he hit you, my dear? You can tell me anything,' he heard Maa plead to his sister one evening as he hid behind a door in the hallway.

'Who have you been speaking to Maa? Who's been spreading these rumours,' his sister asked.

Arif's ear twitched during the uncomfortable silences.

'Of course, he loses his temper sometimes. I mean, it's normal for men to have bad moods and a hot temper, isn't it?'

Arif heard his mum sigh.

'He never behaves badly with me, he never even yells at me,' his sister continued.

Arif knew that was a lie. He had seen his brother-in-law shout at her many times, even when he had invited them around for meals. He seemed especially critical and cruel during those meals because that way he could hurt Maa as well.

Arif had once visited them for a few days and was given a small, comfortable guest room. His books and pencils were still strewn across the small desk next to the bed as he eavesdropped as usual, while his sister and brother-in-law talked in the room next to his.

'Arif is in Year 9 now and he still wears his shorts every day,' his sister said.

'So?' his brother-in-law grunted.

'All the other boys his age wear trousers and I think Arif should also have trousers. If you give me some money I can go down to the market and buy some material and take him to a tailor. Arif is small. It won't cost much for new trousers,' his sister said.

Arif buried his head into his pillow. He felt his cheeks going red.

His brother-in-law spoke. His voice was loud and clear so there was no mistaking what he was saying. He sounded furious.

'Today, I'll buy trousers for Arif, tomorrow I'll buy something for another one of your siblings. The next day I'll buy for your mother. Do I have to take responsibility for your whole family? When are we going to prioritise building our own family?'

'I didn't realise your family was so poor when I married you. You are from a family of beggars. Why is that beggar kid even sleeping in our house?'

'Arif didn't ask for pants, so how can he be a beggar? I just wanted to give him something nice, even if it was small and practical. Why are you telling me off?' Her voice was broken.

'Shut up beggar. Your family didn't give us anything during our wedding and now you're emptying my pockets. When you argue with me, you sound especially stupid, so please shut up,' he said.

Arif wanted to run into the adjoining room and say, 'I don't need new pants. I'm fine with what I have.' But he realised he could appear even more desperate and bring even more shame on his sister. Besides, Arif was terrified of her husband and was not sure of what he was capable.

When the house went quiet, Arif rolled from his stomach to his back and looked through the blue mosquito netting and out the window. The windows were divided into four panels by old iron frames painted a deep green.

Above the window, standing upside-down on the eaves of the roof, Arif saw a small house gecko which turned its head to stare him straight in the eye. They held an unbroken gaze for what felt like minutes as Arif's chattering mind retreated into silence. The lizard licked its eyes, one after the other and scuttled away.

Arif remained transfixed and wondered if a lizard could understand human emotions or did it feel lizard emotions that Arif would never understand?

The sound of Nira's voice reminded Arif that he was still 'hiding' in his dresser and daydreaming instead of eavesdropping. He wondered what he had missed as he walked out shrugging his shoulders to release some tension and took a few steps towards their vanity suite.

'*Some massage,*' he thought, feeling a sudden pang of guilt. He was tenser than ever.

He entered the ensuite bathroom, which Nira had designed to be large, airy, and very functional. As he washed his hands in the big white sink, he looked at his reflection in the enormous mirror that took up most of the wall. He amused himself by making movie star faces and raising his eyebrows in quizzical expressions. As always, he soon forgot what he was doing in the first place.

When Arif realised the tap had been running all this time, he turned it off shamefully and looked back at himself in the mirror. He liked how the appearance of his face changed when he looked in the mirror at different times of the day. The current muted light suited him, he decided, and because he shaved every second day and tomorrow was his date with the razor, his stubble had shot back, giving him a convincing five o'clock shadow. Most of his stubble was grey now and anytime he paid it any attention it looked greyer and greyer.

Arif was not worried about ageing and he assumed the grey hair had something to do with his good health. He felt lucky. The rest of his family suffered terribly from seasonal allergies; Nira and his daughters all became zombies with hay fever during Spring and Nira was allergic to house dust as well. But he remained relatively unaffected by the changing of the seasons.

After washing his hands and face, Arif sniffed his forearms for the slightest trace of massage oil and proceeded to dry himself on a small red towel, which he also sniffed, causing him to gag. It still smelled. Arif scrambled out of his clothes and into the shower, taking the small towel with him. He scrubbed himself furiously for a few minutes before he turned off the taps, the hot one last, and inhaled steam deep into his lungs.

Arif put his clothes back on, hoping that they were not tainted in the small amount of time he had worn them and sneaked past Nira as she tried to end the conversation with her mother.

He peeped into his daughters' room as he went down the corridor. He paused for a moment. The youngest, Zahra, was lying on the carpet, drawing on a notepad as her legs swung lazily in the air above her back. The older daughter, Zebin, was sitting on her bed with a stack of pillows behind her and her legs stretched out almost to the end of the bed. *She's growing up fast*, thought Arif. *Soon she'll need a new bed.*

As she typed on the pink laptop that sat on her lap, Arif looked at the desks in the corner of the room and smiled. He had bought them a year ago and they had barely been used.

Those moments before dinner, towards the end of the working day, were the main times Arif and his daughters spent time together, talking and laughing, with a little bit of homework thrown in. These moments were made even more special by the constant possibility that they could be called to the table at any moment. Arif loved walking to dinner with his girls' hands in his.

The dining area was attached to the kitchen and the family room, in an open plan design, a space that took up a significant area of the whole house. This was how Nira had wanted it. They ate on a white granite table with six ornate chairs upholstered in leather. A chair sat at either end of the table with two chairs on each side. The table had to be moved professionally and Arif hoped they never had any reason to move it.

The first time they ate at that grand table, Arif sat down next to Zebin as Nira placed a big plate of steaks in the middle. She looked at Arif as she stood across the table from him.

'Why are you sitting there, darling? I've laid a plate at the head of the table just for you.'

'Why would I sit at the head of the table?' he said. 'Am I a president or a VIP? I must be a rock star.'

He smiled at the girls, but Zahra didn't understand his joke and the Zebin merely rolled her eyes in the way that teenagers tend to do.

'Even if your jokes are terrible, you are still our father and if Maa says you should sit at the head of the table, you should sit at the head of the table, Baba,' she said when she finally stopped rolling her eyes.

'You're like Mrs Melor, the school principal,' Zahra added. 'She always sits in her chair all alone. She not lonely though, she's important.'

Arif laughed. 'You two are getting bigger and smarter, you're talking like mature people.'

'What are mature people, Baba?' Zahra asked.

'Mature person means … you,' he answered as he reached over and tapped her nose gently with his ring finger. Arif and Nira laughed gently.

Zahra narrowed her eyes as her bottom lip quivered. 'Why are you all laughing at me?'

Arif stood up, walked around the table and put his hand on her shoulder as he gently pressed her head to his stomach.

'We are not making fun of you, darling. We are laughing because we enjoy how smart you are becoming. My daughter is becoming my mother,' he joked, as he swept her off the chair and put her down at the head of the table.

'This chair is now reserved for my little mother,' he said, as the girls burst out laughing. Arif nodded his head in satisfaction as Nira gazed at him lovingly.

As the laughter faded, Zahra looked around the room and took on a regal expression and a royal demeanour. *She is taking her new position seriously,* thought Arif.

'All hail our new leader,' Arif cried and the family burst into rapturous laughter and applause, including Zahra. As they clapped, Arif noticed Nira smiling at him with misty eyes.

                          8

rif's breath formed clouds of condensation as he
strolled down the concrete pathway one Thursday
morning on his way to the university library. He
could feel the cold cement draining his body heat through the soles
of his shoes as he walked along the frozen grass beside the path.

As he entered the library, he was instantly greeted by the
smell of books and a rush of warm air. Arif smiled as he
approached the librarian at the reception desk.

'Good morning, Amanda. How are you?' he asked jovially.

'Good morning, Arif. I'm good, thanks,' Amanda smiled as
she glanced up from her computer.

'Is Linda in her office today?'

'I saw her walk in before but I'm not sure if she's busy. Let
me check for you.' She picked up the phone and pressed a few
buttons.

'Hi Linda, Professor Arif is here to see you ...' she said, before
uh-umming twice.

Arif glanced nonchalantly around the library. He was never

sure what to do with himself in these situations or even what to look at, so he looked at everything he could in the vaguest manner possible.

'Okay, I'll send him right in. Thanks.' Amanda lowered the receiver and turned to Arif, 'Go right through.'

'Thanks, Amanda.' He walked to a door on the far wall, knocked twice and heard Linda say, 'Come in.'

Head librarian Linda smiled at him as he entered the room and motioned him towards a seat in front of her desk. Her jade framed glasses briefly became foggy as she took a sip from her coffee mug.

Linda was roughly the same age as Arif, and wore her grey hair short and spiky. She described herself as being hopelessly addicted to books.

Arif understood this affliction well, although he would have diagnosed his version as a compulsion towards curiosity. That was why he was in the library so often and that was how he had become such good friends with Linda. He visited most days, sometimes for a specific paper but mostly to browse journals for interesting articles. Sometimes he sat in a quiet corner and browsed the popular science magazines, enjoying the colourful way they presented interesting information, trying to glean techniques that he could use in his lessons.

'Good morning, Arif, and congratulations,' Linda said.

Arif smiled and shook his head puzzling over her words. 'Hi Linda, what a nice surprise. Congratulations for what, exactly?' he asked, leaning forward in his chair.

'Yesterday you borrowed your seven hundredth item for the

year. 'Your borrowing probably keeps one fulltime librarian employed.'

Arif laughed, nodded his head in appreciation and raised an open palm to shoulder level, in the manner of a celebrity waving to adoring fans.

Linda's office was full of 'stuff'. Of course, there were loads of books, but she also had all sorts of curios and vintage promotional material that publishers sent when they had a new product to flog.

On her desk was a photo of her pre-teenage kids, a boy and a girl sitting on the back of a grumpy looking donkey. Arif liked that picture, it amused him greatly.

Linda removed her glasses and polished the lenses.

'What can I do for you this morning?' she asked warmly.

'Linda, I need some help with something.'

Linda nodded. She was one of those people who really let you know that they were listening, and it was something that inspired Arif's classroom manner.

'I know you offer part-time jobs, returning books to shelves and other duties. How does one apply?'

Linda laughed and Arif smiled.

'It's not for me, Linda,' he laughed.

'That's a relief. When our most popular teacher starts looking for a new job, it's logical to assume that this school is finished.'

Arif felt a wave of pride and then humility sweep over him.

'Tell me, who are you looking out for?' she asked.

'It's for an international student who's having a bit of trouble.'

'Is the student in your department?'

'No, not in my department; she's not yet even been admitted. But she graduated in mathematics in her home country and has come here to study further. It seems to have brought her nothing but misfortune and I want to help her.'

Linda nodded and listened intently as Arif told her the few things that he knew, and the few things he felt he could share about Amelia. He chose his words very carefully.

'Okay, I can offer her work in the library, around six hours a day, three days a week,' said Linda. 'But the problem is that she is still not enrolled at this university and it's our policy that we only offer those jobs to our own students.'

'Thank you, Linda,' Arif said. 'I know this might seem a bit problematic, but very soon she'll be admitted into a graduate diploma program in the faculty of science and then there will be no problem at all.'

'That's okay, Arif. I am happy to help. But this Amelia, she isn't the only one in Australia. There are probably thousands of Amelias in Melbourne alone. How many Amelias do you think you can help?'

'It's only possible for me to help one, because I only know one Amelia. If we can rescue one, we might inspire someone to rescue another Amelia, and then if our Amelia is in the position to rescue another... well, before you know it Amelias could rule the world.'

They both laughed for a moment and Arif glanced through the window at the golden sunlight that was bathing everything and then returned his gaze to Linda.

'Can you keep a secret?'

Linda looked surprised.

'Secrets, Arif? I generally frown upon workplaces that keep secrets but I will make an exception for you because I'm very curious about what you might be about to say.'

Arif leaned forward and lowered his voice. 'She actually works in a massage parlour and seems semi-trapped there. I actually went in to have a look.'

'Wow, Arif. Really?' Linda leaned forward, her eyes widening. 'Oh to be a fly on the wall for that one,' she added with a grin.

'I was curious ... and concerned of course. There have been so many news reports on massage parlours and the problems that go with them, problems that mainly effect the people working there. And there are so many of them in almost every suburb across Melbourne now; new places are opening all the time. Where I live, even five years ago, we had no massage parlours at all. Now there are six or seven of them within five kilometres. What is happening in this city, supposedly the most liveable in the world?'

Arif stopped talking and took a deep breath.

'I'm sorry Linda, I shouldn't be ranting at you first thing in the morning.'

She smiled at him. 'Arif, I'm a librarian. I love monologues. And I trust your instincts... If that's the case and she wants the job, she is welcome to start next week. I just hope we pay enough. I have a feeling she may find a discrepancy in her earning potential starting up at a library.'

'She will be fine here,' said Arif. 'A perfect fit. Besides, I don't think she has much earning potential that's in her comfort zone back at the shop.' He glanced at his wristwatch. 'Are you going to the academic council meeting this morning?'

Linda nodded. 'Of course.'

'I guess we should head down there soon then. It's starting in twenty minutes. I hope I haven't burdened you first thing in the morning, Linda. Apologies if I have.'

Linda sighed and smiled, 'No, not at all. I can see why you are so popular with the students. Not only do you teach them; you have your own dreams for them as individuals as well. That's really sweet.'

Arif blushed and laughed nervously.

'I just teach chemistry, Linda. I don't have that much power. I teach chemistry, environmental chemistry and environmental sustainability. My dream is to inspire them to put these concepts together and contribute to the fields of sustainable production and development. Our generation is undermining future generations abilities to meet their own needs, so these kids need to develop their own systems to negate the damage that we've already done. As a member of an older generation who is handing the world to these kids, I feel some responsibility for their futures. And the outcomes for the whole planet, I guess. Anyway, I am far too mentally animated for this time of day. I seem to be ranting again.'

Linda laughed, 'Arif, as I said, you can't bore a librarian with ranting. Your passionate monologue was inspiring on such a cold morning, especially before such a boring meeting. We should grab a quick coffee and a cup of tea before it starts. I've got tea bags here as well that you are welcome to use.'

'Thanks, Linda, but we still have time. Let's go to the cafeteria.'

'Good,' she said. 'I'll let Amanda know that I'm going to the meeting.' She held her office door open for Arif. 'After you.'

The campus cafeteria was one of Arif's favourite places. It refreshed and energised him but not with its food, which was as ordinary as you could buy at the train station across the road. It was the buzzing atmosphere of having so many students in one place that electrified him.

While writing a research paper or analysing results from an experiment or when he was stuck in his office feeling his brain drain down to nothing, he often energised himself in the cafeteria.

The cafeteria was on the ground floor of the building next to the library. Most of the common areas were clustered together in the centre of the campus like the nucleus of a single cell organism. The various specialised academic buildings formed a ring-like membrane around the common areas.

Arif glanced out a window facing the east side of the campus. He could see the oval, covered with lime-green winter grasses. He found this vibrant new growth mesmerising and his favourite seat faced southeast straight over the oval. If he looked left, he could see several eucalypts, now full of red blossom, and a couple of leafless maple trees. These trees created a shady zone where the smokers congregated on a half-circle of benches around an old office-size, coffee tin; the communal ashtray which also served as a skills test as the students tried to fling their butts in.

Arif loved to surprise students by walking up to the area as they smoked on the benches. He enjoyed seeing the puzzled looks on their faces. He remembered approaching a student he knew quiet well, a third year named Steve.

'Do you mind if I sit down with you, Steve?'

Steve looked at him confused almost befuddled, as he fiddled with the brim of his faded red baseball cap.

'Not at all, Arif. Sit down,' he said. 'But you do know this is the smoking area.'

'In that case. maybe you could give me a cigarette, please? Only if you have enough, of course, I know they're not cheap these days.'

'Yeah, of course,' said Steve, grinning. He reached into his grey tracksuit pants and offered him the pack and a lighter with one hand.

'I didn't know you smoked,' he added.

'I was a student once, too,' said Arif, speaking out of the corner of his mouth while he lit the cigarette like a cowboy.

'These days, I don't smoke very much. But sometimes I see students puffing away and I want to join them. Anyway, thanks Steve. I appreciate it.'

Arif liked walking into the smoking area. He didn't judge anyone. For him it was just another space for the collision of young minds.

⌒∽⚬∽⌒

Arif led the way to the cafeteria where they were greeted by a tattooed young man behind the counter. 'Hi Arif, what will it be today?'

'Hi Stu, a regular cappuccino with one sugar for Linda and an English breakfast tea without any milk or sugar for myself.'

Arif paid and stood to one side while the young man prepared the drinks. Arif took them over to the table that Linda had saved for them.

'Thanks for the coffee,' Linda said, as Arif took a seat opposite.

'It's okay. My pleasure.' He blew on his tea to cool it down as he closed his eyes for a moment. All he could sense was joyous shouting and animated chitchat and all the other noises of youthful energy. *What a wonderful environment*, he thought.

'What are you thinking about now, Arif?' asked Linda.

'I'm thinking about an article I want to write, an article for young people.'

'What's it going to be about?' Linda sipped her coffee and leaned forward.

'It's going to be about how our generation are all talk and how they need to take the power from us, once and for all. We're screwing them over completely,' said Arif, quickly.

Linda lowered the coffee cup from her lips as she started giggling.

'Sorry,' Arif said. 'I think the energy of the cafeteria really affects me.'

'Ha-ha, but you're right,' she said. 'If you heard me mouthing off at the pub on a Friday night, you'd probably never speak to me again.'

They both laughed and finished their drinks.

'Time to go?' asked Linda.

'Time to go,' agreed Arif.

Arif found himself insanely bored for much of the meeting. He had an insistent headache that wavered in its intensity as the morning dragged on. At its worst it felt like there was a drone flying in circles around his head.

He figured it had something to do with the lights. In Australia, no matter how bright the sun was outside, people working indoors always had the lights on. Most of the lights were dull florescent tubes that gave off a life-sapping glow. Arif felt the lights denied him the chance to feel the natural rhythm of the day. A denial of nature itself. Such a travesty.

Arif looked out the window and craved unimpeded sunlight without any artificial light filtering it. Even though they had a long break for lunch, which was professionally catered with trays of mini sandwiches and fruit platters, Arif felt exhausted by the time 2 pm came around and the meeting finished. He said goodbye to Linda and the rest of his colleagues.

He walked out of the building and stood on a grassy area with his face in the sun. The first semester was over and there were still three weeks of holiday left until the second semester began so there was little work that needed to be done. There was a thesis that needed to be reviewed, but he'd already started on that and there was plenty of time to submit his reports.

Instead of going back to his office Arif decided to go straight to his car, hoping he could beat the traffic.

Arif found the turn-off to the freeway then the exit to the highway. The drone was still somewhere near his head, but sounded more distant now. The rhythm of driving had taken its buzz away. He turned into an exit lane on the left and on to a two-lane road and drove a small distance until he pulled up to a red light. When it went green, he drove a further two hundred metres and pulled into the service lane.

On the left side of his car, a set of suburban shops flitted by. They were like any other, off any other service road, in any part of Melbourne. There was a bakery, a dry cleaner, the obligatory fish and chip shop, and a newsagency that also served as the post office where elderly people paid their bills. Arif found a parking space in front of the pizza shop.

Three bored looking men in tracksuits and aprons sat at the table out the front, smoking cigarettes and drinking cans of Coke. They watched his car pull up next to their shop. They must have been relaxing between lunch and dinner service.

Arif stepped out of the car.

'Pizza, bro?' one of the young men asked in a bored but friendly tone.

Arif looked in their direction.

'No thanks, fellas,' he told them, 'I'm just stopping for a massage.'

The youths clapped their hands and laughed.

'Yeah, brother,' one said. 'You're all right, bro.'

Arif instantly regretted his attempt at impressing the youths. He hoped his family never came to this pizza shop. He smiled at the young men and upped his pace.

'If you get hungry after your "rub and tug", stop in. We'll feed you good, brother,' the man said.

Arif suddenly felt sick hearing what they called it. What a horrible name.

'Great, thanks fellas,' he replied.

He walked with extra determination, down the street and towards the shop, nervously glancing around, making sure no one he knew was in sight.

Amelia had just seen her fourth customer of the day and was drying herself next to the basin after washing the oils off her arms. She grabbed a steaming hot rag and put it over her face for a few moments, running it down her forehead and her nose. She buffed each cheek before walking through a door to the girls' waiting room.

The waiting room had one other door that led to the reception desk where Amelia greeted customers entering the shop. Amelia sat down on a dirty old leather couch that looked as if it had been rescued from a tip. It may have once been white, or close to, but now it was the colour of coffee stains and dirt.

She pulled her knees close to her chest and shivered slightly. Her breath condensed in front of her face, reminding her how annoyed she was that there was no heating or air-conditioning in the staff room, whereas the massage studios were climate controlled or close to.

She took out her phone and mindlessly scrolled through her notifications. Apart from the couch and a bench, the only items in the room were an electric kettle, a microwave that hardly warmed anything and a dull steel sink. The appliances had been there so long they'd turned the same colour as the couch, and they seemed to be there for looks only as the girls were discouraged from eating at work to avoid having distracting smells drifting through the shop. Amelia looked up suddenly as she heard the chimes on the door start to jingle. She took a small vanity mirror and a lipstick from her bag and checked her makeup before hopping to her feet and walking into the reception area.

She recognised Arif's back, as he stood looking nervously through the glass of the front door.

'Hi Arif,' she said. 'How are you today? Have you decided you like massages again?'

Arif forced a booming laugh, 'Hahaha. I'm good, thanks Amelia. How about you?'

'Yes, I'm good too, thanks. What will it be?'

Arif removed two fifty-dollar notes from his wallet.

'One hour please.' He handed her the notes. She nodded politely and led him into the corridor, holding back the curtain for the first studio to the left.

'Go inside and I'll be back in a minute,' she said.

Arif shrugged and entered while she went to collect some towels and a basin. When she returned, Arif wasn't sitting on the massage table as usual. He was seated on a small, armless chair in the corner of the room. He had removed his shoes, which were lined up beside him.

She put the basin and towels on the table next to the massage bench and stood in front of him, with a hand on her hip. She could smell his cologne drifting up to her nose. It was a smell she could now recognise. It somehow cut through the smell of patchouli and sandalwood.

'You have to lie on the table,' Amelia said. 'Otherwise, how can I massage you?'

'I'm not getting a massage today,' Arif said in a casual tone.

'But you paid for an hour.'

'I don't really like massages.'

She crossed her arms and looked at the massage table. She paused a moment before slowly turning to face him.

'Maybe you want a different kind of massage, a special one, but you're too shy to say? You don't have to tip me today. You have tipped me enough. If you want me to, I can take my top off? Or do you want to see my panties?' she asked him, intensely.

She stared at Arif, who seemed relaxed.

Amelia moved to stand beside him and rested an arm on his shoulder. She let it slide around his back as she sat on his lap, pushing her breast into his chest. She lifted her head, so her mouth was centimetres away from his ear as she yanked his shirt out of his trousers and placed her hand beneath it, combing her fingers through his chest hair. He still wasn't reacting. Maybe he had stage fright? Or maybe he'd had a sudden burst of sexual confidence? She kept on rubbing.

'You can kiss me on the cheek if you like,' she said.

She worked her hand back down his chest, over his stomach until it was touching the rim of his pants. She felt Arif grab her hand.

'Please stop,' he said.

She pulled her hand away and he gently loosened his grip.

'I haven't come for a special massage either. I'd like to know you as a friend.'

His statement baffled her. 'Why do you want me as a friend?'

'You know what? I don't even know why. I don't usually seek friendships with young women. But you've triggered my curiosity and my curiosity gets pretty intense.'

'So, you want to become friends because of your curiosity? That makes no sense to me, Arif,' she said matter-of-factly.

'Curiosity because I want to help. Curiosity cannot be denied, at least not in my world. Our ancestors thrived on curiosity and from curiosity all the great discoveries of the world were made.'

Amelia laughed lightly. 'And where do you see your "curiosity" taking you, Arif? What great discoveries do you envisage from my friendship?'

'I'm not sure. My curiosity doesn't give me the ability to see into the future.'

'So, you're curious enough to seek my friendship but you have no interest in my body… or my touch?'

Arif nodded.

Amelia bent down and took Arif's ear lobe between her lips. She let it slide out and purred into his ear.

'I love curiosity. I'm a very curious person too,' she whispered.

Arif jumped up and started laughing loudly. His hand shot up to the ear she had been fondling. Amelia instinctively stepped back out of the way.

'What is it? What happened?' She turned her head towards

the exit, straining to hear any reaction to the commotion she'd caused.

Arif's face was still bright from laughing. He finally stood as Amelia moved in front of him, awkwardly. He gently laid a hand on her shoulders.

'When you were talking with your lips in my ear, you said something that made my eardrum buzz like a bumblebee; it felt like you were tickling me. Sorry, I have a very ticklish body,' he said, smiling softly.

Amelia felt a giggle start in her throat. They both laughed and Arif took a step back.

'You could have taken anything before, more than almost any other customer before you. Why didn't you? Are you trying to be a saint? Is this how you train yourself?' she asked, with her hands on her hips.

Arif laughed.

'I was curious enough to let you carry on for a while longer, same as with the massage. You are extremely attractive Amelia. But that is not why I am here. And I am not here to be a saint. I've heard the stories of some saints' lives; you'd be surprised what some of them got up to.'

Arif sat back down on the chair and put his shoes on, trying several times to do his shoelaces up before he finally succeeded.

'What, you're not leaving now are you? Not even fifteen minutes have passed. You said that you would be here for an hour. If someone is watching the shop and sees someone come in for only fifteen minutes, I could get into trouble.'

Arif stood up and stepped forward, before sitting on the

edge of the massage table.

'I want to tell you something, Amelia.' he said.

She stepped forward instinctively.

'But ... would you meet up with me another day?' Arif asked timidly.

'What do you want to tell me? Why can't you say it now?' she asked, suspiciously.

'I don't want to talk here,' he said. 'I find it too uncomfortable. I'm not judging anyone, but it's not a natural environment for me.'

'You can still talk, I'm not comfortable in many situations, especially in a new country, but I can still talk.' She paused. 'Do you know that I've never been out with any customer before? Why should you be the first, Arif?'

'Please Amelia, you don't need to be apprehensive. I only want to talk to you. There can be people all around. We could talk in a shopping centre, or a major train station, or we could even talk in a stadium. Have you been to any Australian sporting events? It's football season at the moment.'

Amelia shuffled her foot with unease. She did not want to think badly of this man. Then again, she had been around long enough to recognise he was following classic patterns of behaviour that other well educated, professional, middle-aged customers also engaged in when they visited massage parlours.

They would start off by being modest and softly spoken, freely sharing unwanted advice with the girls, drawing from their so-called life experience. They were often panicky as well, even a little bit rigid. Like Arif, they would come frequently at first, just wanting a chat and to prove their virtuousness. Once they felt that they had established enough goodwill, they would propose a meeting away from the parlour. Usually in a hotel or at their homes when their families were visiting relatives. But Amelia wasn't sure what this guy was up to and couldn't guess what he would tell her. She kept staring at him.

'Okay,' she said, without emotion. 'I'll think about it and text you.'

Arif's eyes and face sagged with relief.

'Thank you, Amelia. You really are very smart and intelligent. I've got to go now.' he said.

He got up from the massage table and took a couple of fifty-dollar notes and a business card from his wallet, placing them on the crisp white sheets.

'I will be waiting for your text. See you then. But of course only if you feel comfortable.'

He walked out of the room. Amelia stood where she was for a minute. She felt stunned until she heard the jingle of the door chimes and the door close. Her brain exploded with thoughts but nothing she could hold on to or connect. She looked at the two fifty-dollar notes.

What did he want? Did he want a travel companion for an overseas trip, maybe to a science conference at a prestigious university? Amelia realised she had many unanswered questions about this strange man.

As she lay in bed later that night with the lights off, she grabbed her phone and went into her messages. She took Arif's card out of her purse and entered the numbers into her phone before she typed out her message.

'*I can meet you at Melbourne Central, next Monday 1 pm. A.*'

95

9

Arif was in the bathroom when Nira walked up behind him and caressed him from behind. She looked over his shoulder into the mirror and into his eyes.

'Shaving in the morning, Arif?' she said, happily. 'You normally shave before bed and leave bloodstains all over my pillow slips. This is a nice change.'

Arif smiled back at her, also via the mirror.

'Is it, Nira? I sometimes shave in the morning. And I'm a skilled shaver. I'd never draw blood on your linen.'

Nira cut him off. 'Humming as well. I could even make out a discernible melody .So why are you so chirpy on a Monday?'

'Chirpy? I don't know about chirpy, but whenever I go to work by train and don't have any classes I feel more relaxed.'

Arif paused as he turned on the tap, rinsed his razor and continued shaving.

'On the train I can glance out the window at the passing scenery or look at what other passengers are reading or wonder what they are doing on their laptops. But the best thing is that I don't have the hassle of driving.'

'That does sound nice,' said Nira. 'Please make sure you have something healthy for lunch, Arif. No fried food, please.'

Because he was catching the train, he had asked Nira not to make him any lunch. He tried to take up as little room as possible when he rode on trains. Just him and his briefcase. Nira's intricate lunches always required a bag of their own.

'Why can't I eat fried food? I have no problems with my digestion and it's the same food just cooked in oil,' he complained.

Nira folded her arms and gave him a comical glare as he turned on the tap and rinsed his razor again.

He gave his wife another smile. 'You know, Nira, I think you're starting to develop a bias against delicious food in your old age.'

'Arif,' exclaimed Nira with feigned shock.

'It's okay, Nira. I'll have a lean chicken sandwich or something. You know I was only joking.'

'Try to find a healthy one,' she said.

'Of course,' said Arif meekly.

'And, please, when you get home tonight, can you not go straight to your study?' Nira lowered her voice. Arif flashed her an inquisitive look as she continued.

'The girls are still on holidays and they're going to help me with dinner. We're cooking those steaks we got from the butcher on Saturday and they're preparing dessert all on their own.'

'Hmmm, yum,' said Arif with an obvious hint of concern.

'They're making a special surprise for you,' she said, dipping her eyebrows. 'And I was thinking that after dinner we can all sit down in front of the big screen and watch a movie together. We haven't watched a movie as a family for a really long time. They've already got a movie in mind so try to be enthusiastic.'

'Does it have to be tonight?' Arif asked, glumly. 'I need to review some research papers and there are work deadlines pending as well ...'

'Do it for the girls, Arif. Surely, it will not make any difference to your career in the long run if you spend one night with your family.' Her words ushered in a shared moment of contemplative silence.

'Okay, okay.' he said, smiling at her through the mirror.

He turned quickly and touched Nira's chin with his left hand, lowering his face and lining up his lips with hers. Nira put a finger over Arif's mouth and turned away, laughing as she ran out the door.

'You know, Arif,' she called from the other room, 'I think you're starting to slow down in your old age. Soon you'll be too old to steal any kisses at all.'

Arif had arranged to meet with dean at 10 o'clock that morning. He had four big research projects under way and, because of his position, Arif was the team leader on all of them. It was a lot of work and responsibility in terms of the students who were studying for PhDs and fellowships so he wanted to ask the dean if he could hire a part-time data analyst to ease the workload and handle some of the more mundane chores.

The meeting was brief and uneventful but eventually

successful. Arif just needed to fill out a few forms and his request would almost certainly be granted. They shook hands and Arif returned to his own office to complete a few things before he went to his second meeting for the day.

First, he made a call to the recruitment officer to find out the prerequisites for students to be admitted into the graduate diploma program. Next, he loaded up the staff portal and printed off student enrolment forms, a student enrolment guide and the course brochure. He glanced at the time in the corner of his computer monitor and saw that it was half past eleven. Almost time for him to leave. Arif set his computer to sleep, gathered his papers and put them in his briefcase.

It took less than five minutes to walk to the train station where he waited on the underground platform. It reminded him of a cold concrete bunker. The city-bound train soon arrived. It was almost empty at this time of day. He sat across from an elderly woman, dressed in black with a vinyl shopping pram beside her. They shared a respectful nod as he took a seat next to the window, resting his briefcase on his lap. As the train started moving, he turned to stare at the hypnotic parade of passing scenery — and random thoughts started swirling through his head.

When he had first arrived in Australia, Arif had assumed that Melbourne Central was the main station servicing the central business district of Melbourne. It was only after a few years of calling Melbourne home and travelling through the City Loop on many occasions that he realised the station called Melbourne Central took its name from the vast shopping centre above it. Flinders Street was Melbourne's main train station and had never been surpassed by newer developments.

The train was almost full when a woman's recorded voice announced that the next stop was his. The train glided to a halt and Arif strolled off the carriage, gripping his briefcase as he worked his way through the crowd of students and elderly people.

After taking an elevator up to street level, he approached the barriers and touched his travel card against a sensor. The barrier flipped back with an awkward clunk and he entered a grand food court which had a carnival-like atmosphere at that time of the day. Students and workers were swarming in for lunch and staff struggled to get orders out as quickly as possible. The aroma of different cuisines filled his nostrils and he stood transfixed for a moment taking in the full spectrum of appetite inducing smells until he felt a vibration in his pocket and fished his phone out.

It was a text message from Amelia. *I'm under the big clock.*

Amelia waited under the big timepiece at Melbourne Central Shopping Centre. Of all the places in Melbourne that she was familiar with, this was the most public. She had let her friend, Busarin, know where she was, which seemed a sensible precaution when meeting a strange man. Her experiences in the massage parlour had made her wary and the fact that Arif was obviously over forty and had set up a meeting with a young woman could not be ignored.

Busarin, who had the day off from uni and lived in the city, was going to show Amelia her favourite shops once she had finished her meeting with Arif.

Amelia looked up and saw Arif walking through the crowd, heading in her direction and swinging his brief case. He was wearing a blue collar over a jumper that faded from maroon around his neck to orange down near his waist. The effect reminded her of twilight. She waited awkwardly, constantly changing her gaze from side to side.

'Hi Amelia, how are you? I hope you haven't been waiting long,' he said, as he stood next to her.

'I'm good thanks, Arif. I have only been here a few minutes. How are you today?'

'I'm good, but a bit hungry. Have you had any lunch yet? Can I buy you something?'

'I'm fine, thanks. I had a big breakfast.'

'At least let me buy you a tea or a coffee?'

'Okay, that's fine, thanks,' she nodded back.

'I don't really know this place very well. Are there any good spots for coffee nearby?'

'I'm newer to Melbourne than you,' she said. 'But the city is famous for its coffee. There must be a coffee shop around here somewhere.'

Arif glanced up at the clock and sighed.

'It's such a beautiful clock. Do you know what its special feature is?'

'No, I'm not sure,' Amelia answered, slightly confused by the question. 'It looks like a giant version of one of those watches that elderly men wear on chains.'

'A fob watch,' Arif exclaimed with a finger in the air.

He suddenly looked very much like the professor he was.

'Well, it is big and it certainly tells the time, but it puts on a show as well. Every hour, a section slides down from behind the clock and clockwork puppets of native birds start flapping their wings as clockwork musicians play *Waltzing Matilda*,' he told her.

Arif paused in contemplation.

'Do you know that song? The one called *Waltzing Matilda*?'

'No, is it an Australian song? I'm not even sure what those words mean together,' Amelia grinned.

Arif laughed.

'It is an Australian song,' he said. 'I don't even know if many Australians know what the title means. I've been through the station here so many times, but I never knew about this clock until my daughter sent me a video.'

'You have a daughter?'

'I have two daughters.'

Their conversation came to a sudden halt. Arif scrambled to get it restarted.

'It's good to see you outside of the massage parlour, Amelia,' he said. 'You dress well.'

'Thanks for the compliment. You look good too; you look younger.'

Arif shrugged and grinned at Amelia's backhanded compliment.

'The company of young people is infectious,' said Arif. 'Maybe that's why I look young. Let's find a coffee shop. In forty minutes, it will be close to the hour and the whole spectacle of the clock's performance will start. I would love to see it for real.'

'I'm as curious as you, Arif. Your curiosity must be contagious,' she said as they walked past the entrance of a fashionable café.

'Maybe we can go in here?' Amelia suggested.

'It looks fine to me,' said Arif.

They entered a small café, which looked like a caricature of minimal modernism. The white walls were scattered with blocks of orange and black, seemingly at random as they followed no discernible pattern or logic. The tables looked futuristic, like they were moulded out of a strange ceramic, and the chairs were simple orange and black vinyl-covered cubes.

They craned their necks in search of a place to sit and Amelia pointed towards the back of the room where two people were standing up, gathering their coats.

'I'll save us that table,' she said, pointing towards it.

'Good idea, I'll go and order. Are you sure that you are not hungry? You'll probably feel ravenous once you see other people around us eating.'

'No, really, I'm fine,' she said.

'Okay, but what will you drink?'

'A cafe latte with one sugar, please. Thanks, Arif.' She walked towards the table, stepping aside so the previous occupants, a man and a woman in neat office attire, could exit.

Amelia watched Arif approach the counter and study the perfectly decorated cakes and pastries in the glass cabinet in front of him. She recognised apple crumble, vanilla slice, baked cheesecake, and various other cakes and slices, displayed almost as if they were part of a jeweller's collection. Arif seemed mesmerised by the choice and was holding up the queue until the woman behind the counter interrupted him.

While he placed his order, Amelia pulled her phone from her bag and sent Busarin another message.

Cubist café, near Swanston Street exit.

Even before she could look away, Busarin had replied, *OK.*

Amelia returned her phone to her bag as Arif walked towards her with a sign displaying their table number, 9. He placed it in the middle of the table and sat on an orange cube.

'Our order will be here soon.'

He smiled at her, 'How funny are these tables? They remind me of the décor from *Star Trek.*'

Amelia nodded in agreement.

'This isn't so strange for me,' she said. 'We have plenty of unusual novelty cafes in my country. Asian youth like this style.'

'Where is your hometown, Amelia?'

'It's far from here,' she replied, avoiding any eye contact.

Arif flipped the lid of the vintage water bottle in the middle of the table and poured two half-glasses, one of which he slid in her direction. He took a sip of water.

'Do you like working at the massage parlour? Do they treat you well?'

As she started to reply her throat went dry. She wasn't enjoying this conversation. Why did she agree to it?

'Does it matter if someone enjoys their work or not? People who enjoy their work are lucky. Most people work to survive,' she said.

'That is true, but unfortunate. Could you leave the parlour

if you wanted to?'

'How could I survive if I left? I have no safety net here.'

'Look around, inside this café, outside this café. There are many other cafés and restaurants with so many students working in them, a lot of them migrants like you. They're studying and surviving, most of them only just and it does require short term sacrifice, but it is possible,' said Arif.

'I have committed to my migration agent and I don't have time to get another job. Besides, I am here to study. As you said, the work is a short-term sacrifice.'

Amelia sighed as a male waiter appeared at their table. They stopped talking as he placed their orders in front of them and then removed the table number. He disappeared with a mumble and a smile directed at Amelia.

Amelia picked up her latte and thanked Arif. She used her spoon to taste some of the froth, enjoying the pause in conversation.

Arif looked down at his slice of warm banana bread and buttered it evenly from crust to crust. He gestured at Amelia that she should do the same. 'I hope you like banana bread. I know you said you weren't hungry, but I felt bad ordering only for myself.'

'Thank you,' she said. 'I love banana bread.'

Amelia buttered her banana bread while Arif picked up the teapot and poured some light-coloured tea into his cup. He took a sip as he looked up at his young companion.

'Amelia, I want to provide you with some support. After all, you came here to study, not to give massages and I can help with that.'

'Why would you support me? What do you want in return? Amelia asked. She sounded perplexed.

Arif took another small sip. 'Good question. Why do I want to support you? To be honest, I don't know why. But it feels like the right thing to do. I am a teacher, I enjoy seeing people succeed in their academic endeavours. Surely, that's reason enough.'

He looked at Amelia and nibbled at the corner of his banana bread. He raised it towards her slightly, gesturing that she should also have a bite, before replacing it on his plate. Amelia noticed that he was a delicate eater, taking small bites without opening his mouth too wide. He also sipped his tea silently. She took a small bite from her portion of banana bread.

'How exactly would you support me?' she asked.

'I can set a few things up. For instance, there is a job at the campus library I can help you apply for and there is also another job in data analysis, through our faculty research officer. I have the job description in my bag right here,' he said, tapping on his briefcase. 'With two jobs you could live and study as well and I also have the forms you need to apply for our graduate diploma program.'

'I still wouldn't have the money for a graduate diploma. The fees are too much for someone in my position,' she said. 'Thanks anyway, Arif.'

'How about if I lend you the money... for your first semester at least? Then when you have a good job, you can pay me back, little by little. For the second semester you should be able to save enough from your two part-time jobs to pay the fees on your own and if not, I can help you a bit as well,' said Arif.

Amelia did not respond. She stared down at her coffee, thinking of ways that Arif's plan could work.

'It's okay, Amelia, you don't need to make any decisions right now. Take the papers and the forms, read them and think about it. If this is what you want, fill them out and lodge them with the university. If not, just forget about it. It's okay if you want to stay in your current situation but, please, don't feel too proud to take me up on my offer.'

Amelia nodded as she bit her lower lip and watched as Arif glanced at his wristwatch.

'It five to two.' he exclaimed. 'Five more minutes and the clock show will begin. Shall we go and have a look?'

'I would like to see it,' she said. 'It would be a shame to miss it now we're already here.'

As they stood to gather their things, Amelia glanced at her unfinished banana bread. They walked back into the shopping centre and to the clock, where a crowd of young people, families and pensioners was gathering. People were taking photos on their mobile phones and tourists were shooting videos for their friends back home.

A young couple approached them, wearing the sort of fashionable outdoor gear that identified them as travellers. The male, who was wearing a black puffer jacket, held a small digital camera that he pushed towards Arif.

'Can you take a photo, please?'

Arif took the camera and gestured for them to move together so that the majestic clock face was directly above their heads like a shared halo. The couple's puffer jackets rubbed against each other with an awful scratchy sound as they embraced. They obliged as Arif directed them into a few different poses.

Amelia imagined him in a beret with half a cigarette hanging out his mouth, getting fashion models to pose and speaking with a French accent. The thought made her laugh as she watched Arif return the camera to the young couple and turn back to her with a broad smile.

'Was that fun, Arif?'

'I had fun... and I'm glad that they didn't realise that I'm half-blind,' he joked.

The crowd went quiet and bunched together as the clock hit 1.59 pm. Amelia thought about the manila envelope in her bag and then thought of her parents. Maybe she could be honest with them now? There was another murmur of excitement as the crowd started clapping and counting down the seconds, '10... 9... 8...'

Arif was in full voice, leaning forward with excitement. As Amelia clapped along in time with the crowd she felt an urge to move closer towards him.

As the clock struck two, a hidden panel fell from behind the giant fob watch as magical chiming sounds filled the air. Inside the panel were marionettes of six native parrots, four pink and white, and two white birds with yellow crowns that she recognised as cockatoos.

The birds danced and flapped their wings in a way that reminded Amelia of an old clockwork jewellery box that her cousin owned. It contained two marionette musicians seated in the middle of the panel, playing flute and violin under the watchful gaze of some typically sleepy koalas.

Soon the clock's atmospheric sounds wound their way into a musical theme. *This must be waltzing Matilda*, Amelia thought. She turned to Arif. His eyes were sparkling, his mouth slightly agape. He turned to her and she smiled back.

'Listen to that music. It's so beautiful and otherworldly,' he whispered.

Amelia nodded, smiling in his direction.

'This song is very dear to Australian people. It is often referred to as Australia's unofficial national anthem. It's also the only song I know that's about stealing sheep.'

Arif spoke softly into her ear.

'This whole thing is beautiful, Arif. Thank you so much for bringing me here. But what do you mean, this song is about stealing sheep?'

'It's a folk song about a swagman, which was what they called itinerant workers who travelled from farm to farm with their possessions on their backs. One day this poor and lonely traveller set up camp near a billabong, which is like a pond ...'

'They are very strange words.' Amelia said.

'I think every culture has its share of baffling words. Anyway, as he was boiling his water to make a cup of tea, a sheep came to drink from the billabong and the man captured it for his dinner. The landowner saw him and called the police, who came to arrest the man. But the swagman valued his freedom more than anything and tried to run away. But he fell into the billabong and drowned. Now his ghost haunts the billabong and sings this song.' Arif's voice became spookier and spookier as he went on.

'That's a strange and sad story,' Amelia said.

The animatronic section of the clock slowly climbed upwards, soon to disappear behind the clockface as the last traces of music hung shimmering in the air like an aural mirage. Amelia's eyes felt blurry with emotion as she heard Arif singing softly.

'You'll come a-waltzing Matilda with me.'

10

'This is it, love.' The grey-haired bus driver turned his head towards Amelia and gave her a broad smile. 'Have a good first day.'

'I will, thank you, you too,' Amelia said in a quick set of staccato bursts.

She smiled through clenched teeth as she slung her black gym bag over her shoulder and bounced off the bus. She knew the bus driver meant well, but since working at the parlour she hated being called 'love' or 'darling.' It reminded her of the passive aggressive misogynists who were half her clientele.

Amelia stepped on to the footpath and found herself immersed in the botanical aromas that masked the exhaust fumes from the busy road. Among them she recognised the scent of eucalyptus. But there were others and she smiled serenely as she tried to isolate them, but they were all too unfamiliar. Luckily, they were nothing like the sickly, cloying scents she was used to in the parlour.

The sky was beginning to turn a richer shade of springtime blue and the sun tingled on her skin. Everything looked and felt peacefully beautiful today.

She walked towards a sign that pointed to the campus entrance and turned into a service road dividing the campus into two perfect halves. It was jammed with cars but no one seemed to be in a hurry. She had time to really appreciate the landscaped gardens and lush lawns surrounding the buildings, many of them designed with a low profile to set against the vegetation all around her.

On one of the buildings a giant banner flapped in the wind above its glass doors. Discover Yourself, it said. In conversations with tourists back home, they often told her that they were 'discovering themselves'. It seemed Westerners were obsessed with this idea. She wondered how western civilisation could thrive when it was so inherently self-centred?

Amelia navigated her way through the loose crowd that had gathered. She noticed many different fashion styles and people from various backgrounds. She heard a foreign word or two floating above the din of students excitedly chatting.

Amelia saw her reflection becoming larger and larger as she walked towards the tinted, double doors at the entrance of the building.

This was her first experience of an orientation day in Australia as there had been no streamers, cupcakes or fanfare on the first day of her English course. Everyone wore name tags and that was it. This was in stark contrast to when she was at university back home. She loved her first orientation day so much that she volunteered to help with the activities in her second and third years. She enjoyed welcoming people somewhere, anywhere really; but especially being in a crowd where everyone was full of joy and where the possibilities felt endless.

She opened the tinted door and entered the foyer. She gazed up at the school banners hanging from the high ceilings and walked towards one of the many tables that circled the room. Through the big glass doors that led into the auditorium, she could see stage technicians setting up audiovisual gear around a lectern. Amelia walked past a volunteer with a large box at her feet and green woven bags in her hand. She reached out and handed Amelia a bag.

'Thank you,' Amelia said with a smile.

'No problem. Have a great first day,' replied the volunteer.

Amelia peeped into the bag as she walked to the registration desks. It contained a map, a student diary, a pen, a notepad and various information sheets and brochures. Everything bore the university logo and the slogan *Discover Yourself* as part of its design.

Those behind the registration desks were older than the volunteers who had greeted her, and they all wore blue name tags. Amelia assumed they must be academic staff, although she would not have guessed such a thing had she seen them on the street. She was surprised to see elderly men wearing t-shirts, jeans and sneakers.

When she reached the front of the queue, she found herself facing a man with a wild golden beard wearing a name tag Amelia couldn't fully read. All she could make out was the word

'Prof' with his beard obscuring the rest. The man took off his glasses, wiped the inside of the lenses and put them back on, as he looked up at her.

'Hi there, I'm Graham,' he said. 'What's your name?'

Amelia gave him her full name and he ticked her off a list.

'Have a great day and a great semester as well,' he said.

She breathed a slight sigh of relief as she finally made her way into the auditorium where a big red curtain was descending from the ceiling. Amelia noted that the walls and carpets were also red.

She sat in one of the green and black tartan chairs, in the very centre of the aisle, and thought about the professor. She had never seen such a senior academic wearing a simple polo shirt and jeans. All the teachers in her country were formally dressed and well-groomed; they wore suits, ties, shiny shoes and stern faces. None had facial hair. It was almost beyond a newcomer's imagination to talk to, or even see, a professor or associate professor on orientation day, let alone call them by their first name. This was different but she could see herself liking it.

She glanced at her watch. It was five to ten and the seats were gradually filling up. There were many people inside the auditorium, but surprisingly the noise was far from overbearing and the people around her were talking softly.

Suddenly the red curtain started to rise, revealing a large group of musicians wearing the same t-shirts as the volunteers. She noticed violins, flutes, saxophones, guitars, drums and almost every instrument she knew of. As the band started with a breezy, upbeat, jazzy tune Amelia craned her neck to see if she could see Arif, but he was nowhere to be seen.

Everything he had planned for her had gone without a hitch. She was now enrolled in four subjects, two of which were delivered mainly online, which would allow her to work the two new jobs she had completed online inductions for. Amelia was too distracted and excited to pay much attention to the formalities on stage and soon everyone filed out of the hall for lunch.

On the lush green grass outside the auditorium, the student union had set up a large white tent covered in *Discover Yourself* banners and ticker tape. Smoke and steam flowed out from the tent where volunteers barbecued burgers and sausages. She smelt onions frying and meat caramelising. She walked through the crowd to join the queue where everyone was politely mingling. She saw students with white name tags, teachers with blue ones and others with them in yellow whom she assumed were administration staff. Everyone seemed at ease, which made Amelia feel more comfortable.

She heard a familiar voice behind her.

'Hi Amelia. So you made it here. How is everything going?'

She responded with a smile, 'Hi, Arif, everything's great. This is such a beautiful campus.'

Arif smiled and nodded in agreement.

'I suppose this is the queue for food.'

Amelia nodded in the affirmative.

'Do you mind if I wait with you?'

'Of course not. But isn't that pushing in?' she laughed.

'I'm allowed to.' Arif smiled and pointed at his blue name tag.

Amelia's laughter increased.

'I hope these volunteers can cook,' said Arif. 'Sometimes barbecued meat is a bit raw in the middle and I can't enjoy it very much.'

'I eat anything. Charcoal, blood … I don't care,' Amelia informed him with a wry smile.

The volunteers at the head of the queue stood behind tables, brandishing tongs and serving people as they walked past. It was all very orderly. First, the bread person, then steaming metal trays of meats, then the salads and so forth.

Amelia filled her plate with a lamb chop, a sausage, bread and a chickpea salad. As she waited for Arif she watched him squeeze a little mustard over his sausage and point to an empty bench.

'Let's sit over there in the sun,' he said.

They sat on a bench facing each other and started eating.

'So how is everything going?' Arif asked between mouthfuls of sausage. 'Do you think you'll have any trouble balancing work and study?'

'I'm really having a wonderful day. Everybody is so friendly. And I think I'll be fine balancing work. I'm still not sure what I'll be doing as a research assistant, though,' she said.

'Richard, the manager of our research unit, will explain everything before you start. You'll basically be helping honours students and sometimes PhD students with their data analyses,' Arif informed her.

'Which students will I be seeing?'

'Those who are dealing with large data sets and need a hand sorting it all out. Students who need complex statistical analysis. Some of my students as well. You will mainly be dealing with students from the science and technology faculties. I'll ask Richard to sit with you and explain everything.'

'Thank you, Arif. This still feels like a dream.'

Amelia spoke with a slight tremble in her voice.

'It's really my pleasure. You know I love learning and sharing the gifts of education. Have you learned anything today?'

'I've learned that I like lamb chops,' Amelia said. 'And that mixing chickpeas, mint and yoghurt is actually quite good.'

Arif laughed.

'Ha-ha. See, you are already discovering yourself.'

11

The sounds of cutlery and plates being placed on the table alerted Arif that dinner was not far away, so he went to the bathroom where he washed his hands and splashed some water on his face. Zahra was already seated when he took his place at the dining table. Nira was at the sink, squinting her eyes as she strained the rice in a cloud of steam.

'Where's my big girl?' he asked Nira.

'She's sleeping, Arif. She had a dental appointment today and they put braces on her teeth, remember? She is in bed trying to sleep off the pain, the poor darling.'

Arif felt a pang of guilt.

'I didn't realise that was happening today. I must go and see her before dinner.'

He leaned forward to get up from his chair.

'No, Arif., I'm sorry, but you can't right now,' Nira said hurriedly. 'She's just taken Panadol for the night and might be sleeping. Please don't wake up her now.'

Arif slumped back into his chair, radiating disappointment.

'But how about dinner? How is she going to keep her strength up if she's not eating any food?'

'She had some broth I cooked this afternoon. I think she enjoyed the novelty of drinking it with a straw,' Nira said.

Zahra looked up at him, her eyes wide open and alert.

'Daddy,' she said, 'I don't want to have braces. It looks painful and I don't want it.'

Arif smiled.

'Oh, little one. Not everyone needs braces. Hopefully, your teeth will grow nice and straight. But if you do need braces, it is usually only for a short time and then you will have a beautiful, perfect smile.'

Arif's mouth watered in anticipation of the food to come. Nira had cooked his favourite fish curry with plenty of onions, green chillies and tomatoes. It was the perfect meal. The fish was firm and fresh, the thick gravy was perfectly spiced and it all went perfectly with the dhal, lemon pickles and steamed rice that were also on the table. Nira set his plate down in front of him. Arif always allowed Nira to serve him. Without Nira to compose his plate Arif feared he would starve as his hungry brain struggled with ratios and proportions. The family ate in silence until Nira spoke.

'Arif, I did some banking today and noticed some money missing. Did you withdraw money from the home loan account last month?'

Arif glanced up at her as he took a spoonful of dhal into his mouth. Nira chewed some rice and stared at Arif, waiting for an answer. The awkward sounds of eating suddenly imposed themselves on the silence that enfolded them.

'Oh, yes, I did, Nira. I needed thirty thousand dollars and had to withdraw twenty-five from the home loan account. Sorry, I really should have told you.' Arif made a show of hanging his head in shame, hoping to avoid eye contact for the moment.

'Why are you saying sorry, Arif? If you need it, it is there to withdraw. But I have never seen you use that account before, and I have never seen you withdraw so much at the same time. It seemed strange to me. That is why I asked.'

'I need to hire a research assistant to take some of the workload from me,' said Arif. He popped some curry into his mouth to buy himself a few moments in which to consider his next words.

'It shouldn't be a problem. The university has already told me it would accept my application and reimburse me. In the meantime, I couldn't wait for the slow wheels of bureaucracy to finalise their decision. It would have been too late by then.'

Arif gave a dismissive sweep of his hand.

'Is everything okay at work? You got home late but you don't seem as famished as usual. Is the curry all right?'

'The fish curry is delicious. You really outdid yourself. I really love your cooking. You know that,' he reassured her.

'Then take a little more rice and some more fish. You've eaten very little tonight,' she said.

'I am not feeling good, Nira. I'm feeling feverish and I have a headache too,' he whimpered.

'Arif, you've been complaining about this headache for a long time, now. Don't you think it's time to see a doctor?'

'No need for a doctor. My vision is a little blurry too so it's probably the lenses of my glasses that need to be changed,' Arif said lightly.

'You know everything, don't you Arif. Why don't you open your own clinic and administer your own treatments as well?' said Nira, her exasperation starting to show.

'Give me the clinic's number and I will make an appointment for you.'

Arif nodded.

'Okay. Fine.' He gathered his plate from the table and took it to the sink. He washed it and put it on the rack. Having effectively ended his meal, he left the kitchen rubbing his temples and sat in the lounge while he listened to Nira gathering the remaining plates and cutlery.

Arif sat in silence.

His thoughts were going back and forth. Out of the twenty-five thousand dollars he had withdrawn, twenty-two thousand went straight into school tuition and the other three thousand he gave to Amelia to help her with the incidental costs of becoming a student. When Arif withdrew the money, he had planned on telling Nira that same day, but his anxiety got the better of him and he kept putting it off until he convinced himself that she would not notice. He was not sure why he was so scared to tell her. Nira rarely got mad at him. Arif decided that even though he wasn't technically lying as he really was hiring Amelia as a research assistant. But he was also not telling the whole truth and Nira was good at seeing through such tricks.

Would she understand? Arif was not sure. He felt he needed

to protect her from Amelia, the massage parlour and everything else as well. He decided that once Amelia graduated, he would invite her whole cohort to his home for a casual feast and he would introduce Nira to Amelia and tell her the whole story. Then his wife could be proud of his act of generosity.

Nira entered the lounge and joined him on the couch with two cups of steaming tea. As she sat beside him, he turned to acknowledge her with a soft smile. Neither of them spoke and Arif absentmindedly rubbed his temples.

'Do you still have your headache?' she asked.

Arif said nothing.

'Wait here and I'll get you some Panadol.'

Nira returned to the lounge with a glass of water and a packet of Panadol.

'Here,' she said. She placed two tablets in Arif's open hand. 'Take these and I'll give you a head massage.'

Arif shuddered for a moment, briefly thinking of Amelia. Then he decided to see if this was a massage he could actually enjoy.

Arif lay on the couch, placing his head on Nira's lap and inhaled deeply, savouring her perfume. Suddenly, he felt more comfortable and in his element than he had been for some time. He smiled softly as he let his head fall towards her as he considered the softness of a woman's chest as a child's absolute refuge. He was now a grown man but the bosom was still a safe place. Heaven forbid that anyone, male or female, should ever grow out of such a comfort.

As Nira's fingers began pressing into Arif's temples and

forehead he widened his nostrils and inhaled more deeply until his breath became a rhythm, and he could ride across the gently undulating landscape of his sinking consciousness. As his ruminations faded into nothingness, he could hear Nira's voice and see her words printed across his mind, like ink on papyrus or lights in the sky.

'Poor Arif,' she was saying. 'I love you, my dear,' she repeated over and over again.

Arif was in his office catching up on paperwork on a Friday afternoon, enjoying the quiet mood on campus. When the students were there the place buzzed with energy and excitement, but when they were away, the school took on a different mood, one of contemplation and peacefulness, one where time passed in the gentlest of ways.

Arif's phone began buzzed on his desk in front of him and he reached to pick it up.

'Nira, my darling, how are you?' he said.

'I'm fine, Arif. How's your migraine?'

'It's fine now. Although I need to mark some tests this afternoon and expect that it will come back with a vengeance,' he joked.

'Please don't strain yourself by working too hard, Arif. Surely you can delegate to someone else occasionally,' she implored him.

'Unfortunately, these tests are mine to mark,' said Arif.

'Okay then…. but please don't forget that I booked you an appointment to see the optometrist this afternoon at 5 o'clock.

The same place we went last time. And remember we are going out for a meal tonight so try not to be late.'

'I hadn't forgotten. I will see you afterwards. I'm looking forward to eating out,' said Arif.

'Of course you are, Arif,' Nira chuckled.

To Arif it seemed that Melburnian optometrists were always on the move. How else could the constant turnover of staff be explained? He had been going to the same optometrist for years and had never been seen by the same person twice. There was always a new face peering into his eyes.

As he walked in, a young woman in a white lab coat smiled at him as she walked towards the desk. Her black hair was tied into a tight knot at the back of her head. Arif thought her thickset glasses with bright red frames made her look trustworthy.

'Hi there,' she said to Arif. 'My name is Chen and I'll be your optometrist for today.'

She glanced down at the desk in front of her as Arif looked again at her glasses and wondered how well she could see into the eyes of her patients.

'You must be … Mr Ahmed,' she said in a querying tone as she read the name off the computer screen.

'Yes, I'm Arif,' he said. 'Hi, Chen.'

'Please sit in the chair over here, Mr Ahmed, while I grab a few things and come right back.'

She pointed to a seat in the centre of the shop. Arif walked over and sat down as Chen disappeared through a door bearing a Staff Only sign. She returned seconds later holding a small black case.

She performed every test Arif could remember and some that he hadn't had before. She was extremely thorough in her examination and Arif felt he was in good hands.

'Have you ever had retinal photography performed on you?' Chen asked.

'I'm not sure, I tend to daydream during examinations.'

'It's a simple procedure. We take a photo of your retina to use as a baseline so we can detect any changes in the future.'

'Is there something wrong with my eyes?' Arif asked. 'Is that why I need this new procedure?'

'There's no need to worry. It's a standard procedure these days and something that we now recommend for all patients. I can already see that your eyes are very dry. Dry eyes can cause soreness and headaches as well so I will give you some drops that you will need to use three to four times a day. After you finish them you should come back for an evaluation in three months' time.'

She made adjustments to her equipment and gently guided his head towards it.

'If you can place your chin on this stand and stare into the camera, you will be out of here in no time.'

12

Arif sat in his office tapping a pencil against his desk praying for a distraction. The university had expectations from lecturers and professors with which he was no longer comfortable. He found himself getting impatient with being expected to produce more and more online content and resented the fact that online content was gradually replacing face-to-face time with his students. He was not a multimedia guru.

When Arif first started teaching in Australia most university courses were split into two semesters a year and each semester lasted seventeen weeks. The number of weeks in a semester had been gradually whittled down and he had just been told that from the following year they would only run for eleven weeks. This seemed preposterous, especially for highly involved courses such analytical chemistry or theoretical physics.

How long will it be until each semester lasts for only eleven days? he wondered.

There were other annoyances. Teachers were now expected

to be marketing experts and needed to 'sell' their courses to prospective students to bring money to their institutions. The courses had to appeal to international students who generally paid more than locals but because they often lacked the language skills needed for higher education, they were treated with more academic leniency than local students. He felt as if the courses were being bought, not earned.

Arif feared for the future of teaching now that it was all promotion, marketing and multimedia, and not about a teacher's ability to communicate ideas to a classroom of students.

In the midst of his despair, a pop-up box from his email account appeared on his computer screen. Normally Arif only checked his emails four times a day and now was not a normal time for checking. But he made an exception, needing a distraction. The message was from Professor McCullum and was titled 'Genius.'

'Hi Arif, I thought you'd like to know that Amelia is a bona fide genius. You were right about her talent, my friend. I can't say too much because results have yet to be released but if ever there was a student who came across as masters or PhD material, Amelia would definitely give them a run for their money.
I'd appreciate it if you didn't mention this to anyone, but I thought you'd like to know.
Best regards, McCullum.'

Arif smiled, and decided it was time for morning tea.

Amelia made one of her rare trips to the cafeteria with just enough change in her pocket to buy herself a cappuccino. She rarely bought anything outside of the supermarket, preferring to save her money by bringing sandwiches from home and filling her water bottle at the fountain. Coffee was a luxury.

As her eyes scanned the room from table to table, she saw Arif drinking from a red mug and having an animated chat with two young men. Their eyes met at the same time and Arif smiled at Amelia. He gestured for her to join them. She pointed at the counter and then back at Arif. He nodded and smiled.

Amelia had hardly seen Arif since starting her university studies. There had been brief encounters in the cafeteria and the library, but they were fleeting, a quick 'hello' while grabbing a coffee, or a glimpse while she was stacking books on the shelves.

With a cappuccino in one hand, Amelia approached Arif's table as he flashed her a broad smile.

'Amelia, how are things going?' Arif said as she hovered next to the table.

'I'm fine thanks, Arif. How are you?'

'I'm good. These are two of my students. This is Harry, and this is Michael.'

The three students exchanged pleasantries.

'Do you have a class now?' Arif asked her.

'I've just finished a theory lecture and after lunch I have tutorials.'

'In that case, you should sit down and join us. All three of you have much in common. For instance, you're all brilliant students,' he exclaimed.

Amelia felt her ears and cheeks go red and looked down at her drink. 'Thanks for the invite but I need to meet Linda the librarian. Maybe next time.'

'Of course, no problem. All the best, Amelia. Say hi to Linda for me,' said Arif.

'Thanks, Arif.' She turned to the two students. 'Nice to meet you both.' She gave a polite nod and walked away as briskly as her cappuccino could allow.

Later that day, Amelia found herself walking along the corridor that led to Arif's office.

'Knock, knock,' she said, as she tapped the wood with her fist. 'May I come in?'

'Please, come in,' said Arif.

Amelia opened the door and walked into Arif's office for the first time. She was impressed by the huge window overlooking the ovals and gardens, which filled her eyes with vibrant green. On the opposite wall was a large bookcase with journals and textbooks neatly stacked and itemised, like they were in the library where she worked. Arif gestured towards the chairs in front of the desk where he was seated.

'Please, Amelia, sit down. It's good to see you.'

With only Professor McCullum's office as a precedent, she thought that all university lecturers worked in chaotic spaces with coffee mugs and books everywhere. Arif's office was clean, tidy and functional. Almost minimalistic.

'You would've received your results by now,' he stated.

Amelia nodded and could not help but smile.

'Congratulations. You have done astonishingly well. I believed in you from the start, but you have truly seized the opportunity and excelled. How are you feeling?'

Amelia couldn't prevent the grin and giggle that escaped her. 'I feel good. Really good. Happy and excited and grateful for your help.'

'Have you chosen the subjects you're going to enrol for in the second semester?'

'Yes, I have. Professor McCullum helped me out.'

'Fantastic,' exclaimed Arif. 'Now that you are all set, we should celebrate. You've done so well, I'd like to buy you lunch.'

Amelia blushed and looked at her feet.

'That sounds really nice, but you've already done so much for me, I'd feel bad taking anymore from you.'

'So, you reject my offer as a matter of pride?' asked Arif, teasingly.

Amelia thought for a moment. She could not reject his offer now.

'Lunch sounds good, Arif. What did you have in mind?'

'There are several eating places just outside the campus gate, all within walking distance,' said Arif. 'I am starving. This whole semester has left me feeling famished.'

'You mean go right now?'

'Yes, why not? It's nearly lunch time, I'm hungry and we have something to celebrate,' he said.

'Okay,' said Amelia, with a smile.

'I just need to grab something from my car on the way out the gate,' he said.

'No problem,' said Amelia and just like that they were out the door.

Arif and Amelia sat at a table in the bistro area of the local pub, close to the campus. There were a few people around and she recognised some of the faces as fellow students.

'I've never been to a pub at lunchtime before. Now I feel like a real Australian,' she said and they both laughed.

Arif recommended that they order chicken parmigiana and Amelia's eyes widened when the waitress brought their plates to the table. She had never seen such a thing before. She loved fried chicken, but these pieces were enormous and came topped with sauce and cheese, melted, and browned on top. The chicken sat on a large stack of chips and there was a small side dish of salad.

'Wow, Arif. This looks amazing.'

'Wait until you taste it,' said Arif. 'I'm not a huge fan of chips, but this chicken is really delicious. There isn't much food in Australia that I haven't seen elsewhere, but this seems like a quintessential Australian meal to me.'

Amelia followed Arif's lead. She picked up her cutlery and carved into her meal. It was delicious. She loved the Italian pasta sauce and mozzarella cheese that stretched into strings as she shoved morsels into her mouth. She was eating so quickly she realised if she didn't slow down, she would probably choke on cheese.

'This is amazing,' she said. 'Thank you so much.'

'No problem,' said Arif. 'I'm happy you like it. Also, I've got something for you.'

Amelia stopped eating and looked up.

'Arif, no …'

He cut her off.

'You've done so well, and I know you have no parents or family here to celebrate with, so I've got you a small gift. You really deserve it, Amelia.'

'Arif, I don't know what to say,' she blushed.

'You could say, Thanks,' he replied as he took a small envelope from his pocket and handed it to her.

'I would have bought you something, but I don't know anything about buying gifts. My wife is an expert, but my expertise lies elsewhere. Anyway, please use it to buy yourself something nice.'

'Arif, I can't accept this,' said Amelia, peeping at the envelope's contents. 'You deserve a present more than me. I should buy you something to express my gratitude.'

'No … no, no, no. I am old and I have everything I need That is all yours. Use the money to buy yourself something nice. It's yours to spend whenever and however you please,' said Arif.

13

The optometrist shone a torch into Arif's eyes, blinding him with yellow light as he lay back in the chair.

'How have your headaches been lately?' she asked.

'The headaches are pretty constant, and my vision hasn't improved. I would say that the blurriness has gotten worse,' he told her. 

'Have you been using the drops?'

'Yes, I've been applying them religiously, but they don't seem to work. I still think if you adjust the power of my lenses, we should see good results.'

The optometrist rolled her eyes. *Heaven save us from patients who think they have the answers,* she thought.

'Let's have a look.'

She ran several tests using lenses with various magnifications and charts of different sizes as she examined him with the slit lamp. Arif didn't like the slit lamp. The face-to-face nature of the process made him feel uncomfortable.

She took another retinal photograph and stared at her computer in deep concentration for what felt to Arif like many excruciating minutes but was probably only fifteen seconds.

'When I compare the photograph we took last time with what I took today, I see detectable changes. The colour of the optic nerve behind the retina doesn't look quite right. Healthy optic nerves generally look pinkish, but your optic nerves are looking pale.'

'What does that mean?'

'I can't answer that, sorry. I need to refer you to an ophthalmologist. Do you have any preferred ophthalmologist that you'd like to see?'

'No, I've never been to one.'

'That's no problem. I can refer you to the ophthalmologist group at the Monash Eye Clinic. They have an excellent reputation,' she assured him.

'Do I need to prepare?' asked Arif.

'You don't have to do anything. Just wait. I will send them a referral letter, along with copies of the test results. They will assess how urgent your case is and contact you with the date of an appointment. Do any days suit you more than others?

'Friday is best for me,' said Arif.

'Okay. I will ask for a Friday appointment in the referrals letter.'

She stood up.

'Any questions, Mr Ahmed?'

Arif stood too, following her lead.

'How serious is it?'

'I just run tests and make referrals,' she said. 'But don't worry, you're in good hands. I have referred you to excellent doctors. See you next time, Mr Ahmed.'

She motioned him towards the door and smiled at the next patient, seated beside the reception counter.

Nira appeared behind the front door as Arif retrieved his key and entered the house.

She was anxious and quick with her questions. 'How did it go with the optometrist? Did she change the magnification of your lenses?'

'No, but she did refer me to an eye specialist.'

'Why? What did she say?'

'She didn't know. That is why she referred me, Nira.'

Arif sounded exhausted.

He placed his briefcase beside the sofa in the family room and sat next to Zahra, who was watching TV. Zebin also came into the room, having heard the tension in her mother's voice.

'And how are my two young mummies today?' he asked them, faking a big cheesy grin.

'I'm good, daddy. Mumma said I could watch TV,' Zahra said.

'I'm good too, daddy,' Zebin added. She walked over to give him a hug before going back out of the room.

Nira sat closely beside Arif, their arms pressed against each other's. He detected the smell of mild spices then saw she was staring at the side of his face. Her concentrated look made him uncomfortable, so he bent down to pull up his socks.

Nira was not to be ignored. She persisted. 'Did she give you a reason for the referral?'

'She thinks my optic nerve has turned slightly pale, but she wasn't sure. Anyway, that's a good thing. It's a medical worker being thorough.'

Nira looked at him but said nothing.

'There's no need to worry,' Arif assured her. 'We know nothing at all, not even the doctors do. Besides, Nira, if I lost both my eyes surely you'd give me one of yours.'

He meant it as a joke but Nira looked at him like he was mad.

'Then both of us will be one-eyed, and my one eye will be your eye. Surely you would like that?' he said with a big grin, which served only to make Nira even more exasperated.

'Please, Arif, do you always have to try to be funny?'

Zahra glanced up at him from the TV. She whispered, 'Dad, don't take my eyes. That would hurt.'

Arif laughed loudly. 'Listen to my daughter,' he exclaimed.

Nira turned her attention to the child, who had gravitated towards the television and was now inches away from the screen. 'Sweetie, if you want to keep your eyes healthy, unlike your father's, you need to move back from the television.'

In the second week of the second semester, a letter arrived from the Monash Eye Clinic informing Arif that it had arranged an appointment for him to see an associate professor, Andrew Wathern, in the final week of August.

Nira read the letter in the kitchen that evening as dinner bubbled away on the stove.

'As you don't have classes on Fridays, I guess you could work from home and I could come with you,' she said.

'Why would you want to come? It will be so boring, and the girls need you here,' Arif said.

Nira's response was firm and resolute. 'Don't worry about that.'

Arif was sincere with his reply, 'Okay then, please come and keep me company. I would really like that.'

The second semester of the academic year came quickly and passed even faster. The first semester tended to roll along with a gentle acceleration until a momentum kicked in and everything became intense. Even though each semester was the same length of eleven weeks, Arif considered the first as sterile and polite, but the second was raw and its pace was furious. It seemed to drag and fly past in a contradictory fashion.

The students were hard at work with their final projects, some aiming for PhDs and masters, which meant the teachers and lecturers were busy too. Arif set out at the normal time in the mornings, but during the second semester he rarely arrived home before seven o'clock.

Amelia was also busy. Since she had fled her old flat (and her bond), she had found one closer to the university and was now living with two other international students, Marcia, who came from Brazil, and Amita, who had arrived from India. They all had huge workloads, especially Amelia, who had taken two extra units of physics at Professor McCullum's suggestion.

Arif and Nira waited outside a rough-sawn, wooden panel door with beautiful brass fittings as a light breeze animated the fronds of the tree ferns in the front yard. On the concrete rendered wall, a brass plaque, mounted on the same wood as the door, announced it was the entrance to the rooms of Associate Professor Andrew Wathern.

A distinguished looking, older man answered the door and invited them in. He led them down a long corridor, typical of older terraced houses, and into a spacious office with books lining the walls.

Nira and Arif sat on comfortable wooden chairs as the professor hunkered down behind his desk and scrolled down his computer screen, occasionally checking with papers on his desk. Arif looked around. He noted the red carpet and the dark brown panelling on the walls.

The professor turned from his computer screen. 'How are you today, Mr Ahmed? How have your headaches been lately?'

'Headaches are part of my life now, doctor. It's part of my existence, it's like a second wife,' said Arif, smiling at Nira, who rolled her eyes, before glaring at him.

The doctor shot Arif a little grin before turning to Nira in sympathy.

'And how are you, Mrs Ahmed? Not knowing the details of your husband's problem can be incredibly stressful but we will try to get to the bottom of it today,' he assured her.

'Thank you, doctor.'

'Do you have a history of migraine in your family, Mr Ahmed? Did your parents ever complain about headaches?' the professor asked.

'I'm not sure,' Arif said. 'Whenever they spoke of headaches, they were usually referring to their children.'

The professor ignored Arif's attempt at humour and ploughed on with the consultation.

'I'll get you to do another visual field test, Mr Ahmed,' he said.

'When will that be done?' asked Nira.

'Today. Right now, in fact,' he told her.

He turned to look at Arif and pointed to a door as he spoke. 'You can go to the next room Mr Ahmed. Lisa, our optometrist, is there ready to do your visual field test. After that, I'll perform a few tests myself.'

Professor Wathern turned to Nira. 'It will take some time to complete the tests. If you like you could go next door and get a coffee and sit in the waiting area, Mrs Ahmed. I will call you in when the tests are done and the three of us can sit down together and get a better picture of what's going on. How does that sound?'

Nira sighed and nodded. 'That sounds good. Thanks, doctor.'

After the tests were complete and Arif had a glass of water in his hand, the three of them sat in the office. Arif and Nira stared intently at the professor as he looked from the computer screen to a set of printouts in his hands, and back again. Checking data, making decisions.

'I've got the visual field test report here Mr and Mrs Ahmed and I'll get straight to the point.'

He paused, composing his words. 'These results look ... unusual,' he eventually said.

He laid a printout on the table between them and pointed to the ring of shaded regions around Arif's outer left eye.

'Your peripheral vision is almost completely shaded out,' he said. 'Your right eye is slightly better, but your field of peripheral vision is still extremely limited.'

Arif gave Nira's hand a tight squeeze. 'What does all that mean?'

'It can mean various things. Sometimes these changes happen because of age. As we get older peripheral retinal cells become weak and die. It can also be caused by glaucoma, but I don't see any signs of that so we can rule glaucoma out. If there is a problem in the central nervous system, including the brain, then there may be problems in the optic nerve, so we need to explore that avenue. Your lenses are actually about right,' he assured Arif.

Nira's face looked pale. 'What do we do now?' she asked in a dry voice.

'I'd recommend seeing a neurologist. I can send your file to a neurologist I know well. Do you have private health insurance?'

'Yes,' Arif and Nira said in unison.

'Good. It's well worth it in this case. It's good to get an appointment as quickly as possible. I will ask in the referral letter that your appointments are not delayed,' the doctor said with authority.

Nira and Arif offered him their thanks and left the consulting room in silence.

That same afternoon Amelia went to see Professor McCullum in his office on the second floor of the faculty building. She felt some dismay and she started breaking into a sweat while climbing the stairs. The door to the professor's office was closed so she knocked timidly.

A cheery voice beckoned from behind the door, 'Come in.'

Amelia turned the handle and entered the room.

'Amelia, good to see you. Please sit down.' He gestured towards a chair.

'Thank you.'

She glanced around the room. His desk was a large L-shape. A huge bookshelf started where the table met the wall and rose almost to the ceiling. The furniture was stained a vibrant red and the bookshelves were packed with books and journals. More books and papers were stacked on his desk in a haphazard manner.

Amelia noticed that many of the papers on the desk bore small brown stains. Coffee drips. To his right was the culprit, a large steaming coffee mug that had similar stains running down its side. Also on his desk was a framed photo of his family. Certificates in smart black picture frames testifying to numerous academic qualifications covered the walls.

Professor McCullum finished what he was doing on the computer and turned towards Amelia with a smile.

'So, what's news, Amelia? How is everything going? Things can get stressful towards the end of semester.'

Amelia smiled back. 'I'm doing okay. So far, all good,' she said.

'That's good to hear. Hang in there and keep doing what you are doing. You will get the results you deserve. Which are great results, bloody great results.'

He picked up his coffee-stained mug and took a sip as Amelia leaned forward in her chair.

'The reason I called you here is because I recently submitted a proposal to the Australian Research Council to write a paper on the steady-state conversion of heat to work at the nanoscale. Sounds fun, hey?' he chuckled.

Amelia smiled and nodded. She sat back in her chair, feeling more at ease.

'Well, they thought it sounded fun too,' he continued. 'The project survived the first round and I am hoping we will make it to the end. Assuming we get approval, there will be several research fellowships on offer and I was thinking that you should apply for one. Nothing has been finalised, it is all hearsay, but if the project is approved, my hope is that you would be interested in working with us.'

Amelia sat upright in her chair. 'Well, yes. What would my role be?'

'There's a lot of high-end mathematics in this work. Your skills would be useful to us,' the professor replied. 'You don't have to say anything right now, you've got plenty of time to think it through.'

The following Monday afternoon, Amelia walked along the corridor of the faculty building, lost in a swirl of thoughts and feelings. Exhaustion and excitement were wreaking havoc on her capacity for rational, structured thought. She remembered finishing her final examinations as an undergraduate and leaving the hall feeling refreshing and lightheaded. She was feeling the same today. But excitement and deep exhaustion often created a sense of melancholy in Amelia, and she realised how much she yearned to have loved ones nearby. *God, I miss my family.*

Amelia did a double take when she walked past Arif's office and realised that the door was ajar. Arif was inside. Amelia knocked on the door twice.

'Hello,' she chirped when she heard Arif's voice from behind the door.

'Please, come in,' he said.

Amelia pushed the door open and entered.

Arif stood up immediately. 'Hey Amelia, how are you?'

'I'm good, thanks, Arif. I was walking past and saw your door was open, so thought I would say hello. Sorry that I haven't made an appointment.'

'That's okay, you can visit anytime. No appointment is ever needed. It is good to see you. From what I have heard, you've done even better in your studies this semester. Congratulations.'

'Thank you, Arif, and thanks for giving me the opportunity.' Amelia averted her eyes modestly.

Arif pointed towards a smaller round table on one side of the room, one that he used for informal meetings. He placed two chairs on opposite sides of the table and gestured for her to sit down.

'Let's sit over here.'

'I'm going to get a cup of tea. Can I get you a tea or coffee?'

'Thanks. I'll have tea, with milk and one sugar please.'

'Okay, I'll be right back. There are some journals on the table that might interest you.'

Amelia picked up a journal on physical chemistry but only managed to stare at the pages before Arif returned holding two cups of tea. He placed them on the table and closed the door before sitting down in the chair facing Amelia.

'Now, tell me, how's everything going? How is Professor McCullum?'

'He seems well. He applied to get funding for a research project and part of that includes fellowships. He has offered one to me. He said he'll let me know and that I have plenty of time to think about it. But I don't understand why I feel so anxious.'

'Maybe you need to stop over-thinking it, Amelia. This is a golden, or should I say, a platinum or diamond opportunity for you. Opportunities like this are a one in a million, once in a lifetime event. Anyway, congratulations, that's terrific news. I feel immense pride,' he said, and took a sip of his tea.

'Thanks, Arif. Nothing's finalised yet, it's still only a possibility.'

'If McCullum is already talking about it, he must be pretty certain that it's going to happen. Otherwise, he would not have told you.' Arif paused for a moment. 'I thought something like this would happen, but I did not think it would happen this quickly. It's really wonderful news — try to enjoy it.'

Amelia said nothing. She sat with eyes downcast. Her lips quivered. Arif reached over and placed his hand gently on her shoulder. Amelia looked up and made an effort to smile.

'I feel a little scared and undecided. I don't know why. I want to be happy but I can't shake the feeling that I just want to cry.' Her eyes filled with tears.

Arif studied her closely. 'When there is distress, that's when the tears come… and sometimes people also get tears of joy. At both times, people want to be close to loved ones. But tears also bring the attention of others and create connections that cure loneliness. I am happy that you have come to visit me in my office. My mind was not good before. Having seen you and having listened to your excellent news I feel happy again. Thanks, Amelia.'

She took a deep breath to try to quell her sobs and divert her attention to her mentor. 'Is everything okay, Arif? You look tired.'

Arif glanced out the window before turning back to look at Amelia, who had placed a hand over her face to hide her tears.

'I've got a lot on my mind and I'm feeling a bit stressed. I need to see a neurologist, Amelia.'

There was an awkward pause. Amelia stared at the ground. Her blank mind raced. She felt a sense of panic creeping into her chest. What could she say? What was the correct response? She took a breath and let her eyes rise to meet Arif's as he continued explaining.

'I've received an appointment from the neurological clinic, so it seems more real now. This semester is nearly over, and not only the semester but the whole academic year is also nearly finished. Taking a day off work seems impossible. It's unfair to my students.'

Amelia looked at Arif more intently. 'Why do you have to see a neurologist?'

'It's really … annoying. There is a popular saying where I'm from, that if a tiger attacks or even touches a person, the person gets at least eighteen wounds from the one encounter. The same thing is happening to me with my health. It feels like something is unravelling. I am tired of doing hundreds of tests for my sight. The optometrist referred me to an ophthalmologist, then the ophthalmologist referred me to a neurologist. I keep telling myself it's probably nothing serious, but I don't know. At least I am so busy right now that I don't have time to die.'

'When is the appointment?'

'On the first Friday of October.'

'Is there no appointment before that?'

'Before you came, I was feeling annoyed and filled with boredom; thinking I should be happy because even getting an appointment with a neurologist is like winning the lottery. In that sense I am lucky. But it is in the first week of October. You can imagine how busy we are then. If I tried to move the appointment I would have to wait at least another three months for another one.'

'Are there no other neurologists?'

'It would be the same situation with all the other neurologists as well.'

'Don't worry, Arif,' Amelia said in a comforting voice.

Arif stood up. 'I'm not worried. I'm infuriated. And because of the annoyance, my concentration is deranged. It's the wrong time of the year for these distractions.' He spoke with an intensity Amelia had not seen in him before.

She also stood and moved closer to Arif. They faced each other with only centimetres between them.

'I hope nothing happens to you, Arif. Please... don't be frightened.' Her voice was soft and gentle.

'I'm not afraid, Amelia. If anything happens, it's no harm, no loss. I am ready to accept it.' She thought he sounded so matter of fact about what was ahead.

'Maybe you don't perceive any harm or loss for yourself ... which is crazy. But there will be a loss for this planet and a big loss to your family and friends ... and even this institution and all of your students,' she said.

'And what does that mean, Amelia?'

'I don't know what it means. But if I get the fellowship, I hope that you will be there to congratulate me.'

They remained face to face and eye to eye. Arif raised his hand and laid it on her shoulder.

'Of course, I will be there. My best wishes are always with you, and always will be. Never look back, Amelia.'

Amelia lifted her face and looked at him. The tears pooling in her eyes were about to break through to stream down her face and on to the ground.

'Sorry, I need to go,' she said. She turned away from him and walked out the door.

14

rif and Nira sat on narrow wooden chairs, browsing through the magazines in the waiting area of a consulting room at the Cabrini Hospital. Days earlier, Arif had mentioned trying to change his appointment to another day, but Nira wouldn't have it. Over the years she had heard all his excuses, seen his stubbornness, and occasionally his anger. None of these moods moved her anymore. Arif had even tried pleading. With the end of the semester rapidly approaching the thought of missing a day from work was becoming increasingly untenable. But Nira had made herself clear. She would not allow him to change his appointment, even by a single day.

Arif did not argue. If he did, she would stop talking to him altogether and he hated the silent treatment. He felt such a failure after a quarrel. Nira would only send messages to him via the girls. When dinner was ready, she would ask them to tell him, even though he could hear her from the other room.

An elderly patient came out of the doctor's office followed by a short, well dressed, middle-aged man.

'Arif Ahmed?' the man asked, looking straight at Arif.

'Yes,' Arif said. He stood up and took a tentative step forward.

'Hello, Mr Ahmed. I'm Robert Newsome, your neurosurgeon. But let's not stand on ceremony; just call me Bob. Most people do.'

His smile was warm and welcoming. Arif felt more relaxed already.

'Hi Bob, this is my wife Nira,' he said.

'Hello Nira. Thank you for coming today. If you would both like to follow me, we can go to my office and get started..'

Arif's face was furrowed in thought. The doctor had a presence that Arif found annoyingly familiar, like he was the spitting image of a local politician or a newsreader. Arif shrugged the thought away, followed the doctor into his office and sat down when invited.

It was a typical doctor's office with white walls and anatomical charts placed in the usual places. Arif noticed that, like him, Nira's eyes were scanning the papers and files on the doctor's desk. Her eyes couldn't hide her fear.

The neurosurgeon seemed engrossed in the reports from Arif's previous consultations with other specialists that he had in front of him. He rubbed the sides of his of black-framed, thick lensed glasses and looked at Arif. 'I'm surprised that no one has requested a CT scan. That should have been done before you were sent here. I want you to have a scan by early next week, Mr Ahmed.'

It was not what Arif wanted to hear. 'It's so close to the end of semester. It's a really difficult time for me,' he said.

'I understand that Mr Ahmed, but if something is going on with your optical system, we want to get on top of it so that you are good for next semester, the semester after and many more after that.'

Arif nodded in reluctant acceptance.

'I'll refer you for a CT scan as soon as possible. We could get it done by Monday or Tuesday. I'll ask reception to book us an appointment for Wednesday.'

Mr Newsome stood up. Arif and Nira followed his lead. The surgeon addressed them both.

'Please try to relax until then. CT scans are standard procedure here. It has to be taken seriously but unnecessary worry won't help anyone.'

They nodded their understanding.

'Thank you, doctor,' said Nira.

A few days later Arif visited a medical imaging lab close to his home. He wanted to go alone but Nira insisted she should go with him. He felt like she had become the nurse who stood behind patients while they gave a urine sample. Nira was accompanying him everywhere to make sure he was doing everything correctly.

Waiting rooms had become extremely boring to Arif and he found it hard to sit still. Like most he had been in recently, there were items of reading material on the coffee table and he decided to rate the waiting room on the quality of this material and its curation.

As usual, they were mostly trashy tabloid magazines with a scattering of old *National Geographics*. These were a waiting room staple. It was as if all doctors had a subscription to *National Geographic* in the 1980s and 90s. Arif picked one up. His eyes scanned page after page. No matter what was on offer, he found it impossible not to try to read it. He read anything left in front of him and would even cross the road to read an information board.

Arif felt Nira grabbing his hand and realised that his eyes were closing. He looked straight at her.

'What is it, Nira?'

She smiled at him.

A technician in a blue lab coat approached them and called Arif's name. Arif turned to Nira.

'I'll be right back. I don't think this takes long, it's just a scan.'

'Can't I come in with you?'

'I don't think they'll let you. It's because of the radiation,' said Arif. He kissed her on the cheek and followed the technician who pointed him towards a changing room, where he was handed a white gown.

'Please strip down to your underwear and put this gown on. If have any jewellery or other metallic items, such as a watch, please put them in this tray with your wallet. Once you have done that, I'll be right with you.'

As he got changed, Arif smiled at the memory of the massage parlour the first time he met Amelia. When he walked out of the changing room, shivering with cold, he was directed to lay on a narrow bed in front of the CT scanner, which surrounded one end and made Arif think of a giant white donut. Did he really have to put his head inside that thing. It looked like a lab scale jet engine.

A nurse disinfected a small patch of skin on his forearm

with a freezing cold alcohol swab and inserted a thin cannula. She explained that during the scan, he would be injected through the cannula with a special contrast dye. When the nurse finished Arif heard the technician's voice being projected through a speaker somewhere in the machine.

'We're almost ready to start now, Mr Ahmed. If you would lie as still as you possibly can that would really help, thanks. Everyone, please stand by.'

As Arif lay on the platform, he felt his body being moved into the centre of the scanner. Then came a succession of strange mechanical thumping noises, a bit like a misaligned washing machine but much more sinister. It was a strange type of torture lying still while encased by the scanner. Everything about it made his body want to scream in terror.

The next morning Arif and Nira returned to Bob Newsome's office with Arif hoping he could get back to campus after the appointment. Nira thought otherwise.

'It's Friday,' she said. 'No one goes back to their office after an appointment on a Friday. It's a tradition in this country.'

The neurologist looked comfortable in a light blue shirt with black trousers. A burgundy coat hung from the back of his chair. Arif watched as he placed a picture of the scan over an x-ray viewer.

'Please, sit a bit closer so we can all see,' he said. Nira and Arif shuffled their chairs towards the desk. The doctor pointed to the slide on the viewer.

'What you can see is your brain, Mr Ahmed,' he said softly.

Arif stared at the image like a parent viewing the ultrasound of an unborn child. He had never seen such excellent pictures of himself.

The surgeon gave them a background into CT scans and how the images were interpreted. For the first time he could remember, Arif was impatient while listening to methodology.

'Look at this slice of the brain's frontal lobe. I can see a nodule right here.' Bob Newsome pointed to the slide with his pencil. 'And if you look at the slide with contrast dye, you'll see the nodule very clearly and you'll also notice that the surrounding areas are swollen with edema.'

Arif glanced at Nira. She had gone pale and looked so frail that he was afraid she would blow away.

He turned to face the consultant. 'So, what does this mean?' He heard the trembling in his voice.

'It seems that you have a tumour, Mr Ahmed,' the surgeon said softly.

Arif's ears filled with an awesome, unruly silence, as if he had entered the eye of a tornado. His chest filled with feelings of horror and fear. All three sat in silence and Arif suddenly felt as if there was no air in the room.

He glanced at the windows in a panic and then at Nira. She looked nauseous, one hand firmly grasping a corner of the desk.

'Are you okay, Mr and Mrs Ahmed?' The surgeon's concern was obvious. 'I realise this must be a terrible shock.'

Arif put his arm around Nira's shoulder and pulled her towards him in a solid embrace.

'Please don't worry, Nira. Nothing will happen to me, I promise,' he said.

'Arif is right,' said the surgeon. 'You should not worry, Mrs Ahmed. We still don't know what it is. Besides, a CT scan is not suitable for a proper diagnosis. For that I will need an MRI scan. We will book you in as soon as possible and you can see me soon after.'

'Why do I need an MRI?'

Bob Newsome offered a comforting smile as he answered Arif. 'To diagnose a complex case, there is really no other alternative but to do an MRI. If it is cancer, we are going to need to understand the nature of its location, its size, and its progression. An MRI is exactly what's needed.'

Nira looked at the doctor.

'You said cancer. Are you sure the nodule is cancer?'

'That's what we want to find out by doing an MRI.'

'But why didn't you give him an MRI instead of CT scan last week?' Nira's anger was starting to show.

Arif looked at her lovingly.

'Good question, Mrs Ahmed. There are basic protocols that we follow as medical investigators. It doesn't make sense to expose people to unnecessary tests, both from a safety viewpoint but also in terms of resources. The CT scan was the appropriate scan at the time.'

No one spoke for a few moments. It was Arif who eventually broke the silence.

'Please tell me, doctor, if what you saw in the CT scan is confirmed by the MRI report, then what? Would you be able to cure it?'

The doctor fixed his eyes on Arif.

'I'm sure you understand that the sooner we accurately diagnose what's happening and devise a treatment plan, the better. As a surgeon I am telling you that time is the biggest factor in this situation.'

Arif looked down at his feet, full of thoughts and anxieties, then looked up at Nira. He turned to the doctor, his mind made up.

'Doctor, I completely respect your opinion and the obvious care you put into your work, but I need you to give me three weeks of normality before we start this process. I have many responsibilities and feel accountable for the outcomes of my students. I'm not able to miss work for a single day.'

Nira took a deep breath and the two men instantly turned in her direction. She had the attention of both of them but focused on the surgeon.

'Mr Newsome, I obviously know my husband well and he is stubborn and does whatever he decides. His students' welfare and their academic outcomes are his principal motivation ... everything else is secondary. In the past, I have tried to make him take a day off but he suffers from not being there. That's how he is wired, and I do not want to give him any more emotional or mental pressure. To force him to give up his responsibilities at this time of the year would be a kind of death sentence in itself.'

She paused, an ominous silence filled the room. She took another deep breath before a final outburst, 'I can't tell you how stubborn this man is,' she said, and started to sob.

Arif sighed and placed his arm around her.

'I can't force you to have treatment,' the surgeon said. 'It's all up to you.'

Arif's dull eyes lit up a little.

'Thank you, doctor. I'll be back as soon as term ends.'

The surgeon's face folded into a serious gaze as he tapped away at his keyboard and printed off an MRI request.

'Okay, Arif. Here's everything you need for your MRI scan. I suggest you get it done as quickly as possible so that you can make a timely and informed choice about how you want to tackle this.'

Arif nodded back, thoughtfully.

15

melia walked out of the cold, still air of the examination hall and into the midday breeze outside. In between gusts the feeble spring sun beamed pinpoints of heat down on to her face and her ears readjusted themselves to sounds as they normally were, away from the echoey din of the hall. Her feelings upon finishing exams were always the same. It was a lightheaded giddiness, a taste of freedom and a deep exhaustion that sat in her legs and made them hard to move. The distortions to her sense of time caused by the rigours of student life fascinated her. Only a week ago it felt like time was stuck but now she could not believe how quickly the semester had passed.

Her sense of elation began to fade as she walked through the campus gardens and thoughts of Arif entered her mind. She realised she had an excellent excuse to see him; she could discuss the professor's email with him. She took a deep breath and headed for the faculty building.

As she walked down the hall she became hyper aware of the

sound of her footsteps and the rustling of her jacket. It was her lucky day. Arif's door was ajar and there was no sound coming from inside the room. There was every chance that Arif was alone.

She struck the door twice. 'Knock, knock.'

'Come in,' called Arif.

Amelia straightened her jacket and flicked her fringe off her forehead. She placed her hand on the handle and gently pushed forward. Through the widening gap, she saw Arif look up.

'Hi, Amelia. Please come in.' A cheerful greeting but she detected a tired weakness in his voice.

Amelia stepped inside.

'Are you okay, Arif? Why are you looking like this? Is everything all right?'

Arif smiled, but she thought his exhaustion made him look ghoulish.

'Why? How do I look?' he asked.

'You look like you've lost weight ... you seem exhausted and, no offence, it looks like your age has increased over night.'

'I really am an old man. It was always bound to catch up.' He still smiled, although his lips began to wobble and he suddenly looked down.

'Did you meet with the neurologist?'

'I did... well, I saw a neurosurgeon. He saw my CT scan images and he thinks I have a form of glioblastoma that has spread through my brain.'

Although Arif spoke calmly, Amelia felt the blood drain from her face. She knew English well enough now to know that big words in serious conversations were rarely a good sign.

'What does that mean?'

Arif answered looking straight at her with a deadpan expression. 'It means I have a type of brain cancer.'

'What's the treatment? Is the neurosurgeon really sure?'

'I'm not sure what the treatment is, or if there is an effective treatment. Even famous and wealthy people die of this cancer. I'll find out for sure when the semester is done and dusted.' Again he spoke without emotion.

Amelia stared at him in stunned silence. Tears filled her eyes.

'I can't comprehend why this disease has attacked me. I feel like the cancer has made a mistake and set up its home in the wrong person.'

He gave a nervous laugh.

Amelia pulled up one of the two chairs in front of the desk and sat down. Her hands and feet were shaking, her head was spinning. She felt that she would faint and fall if she stood any longer.

Arif broke the silence. 'My apologies for not offering you a seat when you first got here. You see, I really am becoming an old man. Anyway, how are you? How was the exam?'

'I feel exhausted, but I feel like I did well. I guess I'll see soon enough.' She instantly felt guilty for talking about the future.

'Congratulations. Professor McCullum sent me an email. With the amount of money budgeted it should be a huge project. Have you thought about the fellowship?'

Amelia nodded.

'It's a great matter of pride for the university,' said Arif.

When Amelia offered no response, Arif continued.

'McCullum said there'd be a small ceremony on November 10 when you'll be presented with the formal letter. He invited me as well.'

Although Amelia was still seated in front of Arif's desk, she took in not a word of what he was saying. She couldn't believe what was happening to this person who had lit the light in her current life. Why did life have to be so fragile? Was a person's fate random, or was it a game of God? If it was the game of God, then there seemed to be little justice in the game.

Amelia started feeling nauseous. She stood quickly and fumbled to grasp a corner of Arif's desk. Her sweaty palms gripped it as firmly as possible. It seemed her body and the whole world was wobbling.

'Arif, I really have got to go.' Her voice shook, sounding distant and alien.

'Are you okay, Amelia? You don't look well.' Arif gave an anxious look and stood up so he could put a steadying hand under her elbow.

Amelia took a few deep breaths.

'I'm okay,' she said. 'I'm just exhausted, sorry. Will you be accepting Professor McCullum's invitation?'

'If I can make it, I'll definitely be there. But I have an appointment with the neurosurgeon on the same day, and more or less at the same time. I have already delayed the appointment once. There's no way to book another one.'

'Don't worry, it's no big deal. It's only a ceremony. Seeing the neurosurgeon is much more important,' said Amelia.

Arif spoke softly. 'I never miss this type of ceremony for the faculty. The program starts at 5 pm, right?'

'Yes, 5 pm.'

'My appointment with the doctor is at 2 o'clock. If the appointment ends in time, I will be there straight after. If for any reason I don't make it, please do not get upset, Amelia. I'll be thinking about you and supporting you from wherever I am.'

She noticed a tear well in his eye and felt fresh tears of her own. She looked at Arif with downcast eyes. Words were frozen in her throat. Arif raised his hands and placed them firmly on Amelia's shoulders. She felt herself trembling.

'You've worked so hard, Amelia,' said Arif. 'You've suffered pain and you've cried at night but now it's your time for the success you deserve. My own daughters are too young to understand any academic legacy I could pass on to them but you, Amelia, are at the start of a great journey and I've passed my blue butterfly to you. It's all yours.'

He smiled, eyes shining brightly.

Amelia continued to sob but managed a brief smile. She wanted to speak but was afraid how broken her voice would sound.

'What's a blue butterfly, Arif?'

'A blue butterfly is a dream and a story. It's a journey and a cycle. One day I'll tell you more, although I suspect you don't need me to tell you. You'll work it out for yourself. You always do.'

He lifted his hands from her shoulders.

'You should go, Amelia. I wish you all the best, my dearest young friend.'

Amelia said nothing. She nodded, turned, and left.

Arif felt his heavy eyelids close slowly as he nestled in his seat on the express train home. Nira didn't want him to drive anymore, which he didn't mind. He didn't like driving. His eyes would close, like they were doing now, and if they weren't closed, the late afternoon light would come through the windscreen of the car and give him a headache. These days he felt better with his eyelids shut but he didn't like the idea of falling asleep on the train and a stranger having to wake him when they got to the city.

He muttered and opened his eyes, letting them adjust, before turning his head towards the window.

It was a mild spring afternoon and the blue sky looked fresh and clean. The train ran along a fence line with a row of leafless, gnarled plum trees. They were still bare from winter, except for the countless white flowers that blossomed on their lichen covered branches. Arif found it easy to imagine that each tree was covered in the purest of linen. The last rays of light from the sinking sun gave the flowers a fiercely beautiful intensity and Arif closed his eyes again, preferring to think about the blossoms in the safety of his own brain. Though, now that the inside of his head didn't seem safe, Arif had nowhere left to retreat.

When he arrived home, Arif pulled his key from the front door and let it open slowly. His younger daughter, Zahra, was on the couch reading a book. She would normally come running into his arms, but tonight she hardly moved at all. She lifted her head with a glum look and a hint of fear that broke Arif's heart.

'Hello, little mumma. I love you,' Arif said, as he tried to make eye contact with her.

'Hello daddy,' she said and her gaze instantly retreated to her book.

He looked at the silent, motionless television and turned to walk to his and Nira's room.

Before this dark cloud had descended, the sound of the TV would have assaulted his ears as soon as he reached the front door. The girls would be watching their cartoons at such a high volume that it always seemed that there was a crowd of buffoons in the house, talking and fighting, and carrying on.

He walked quietly past Zebin's room. The door was ajar but she didn't come out to greet him. Maybe she was angry that he had broken her mother's rule.

Nira's rule was simple; when someone arrived home, they were to ring the bell or knock. If anyone was inside the house, the person inside was to open the door. Simple.

Nira said that getting inside by using a key was the same as arriving home to a hotel room, which made Arif laugh. But he knew that this wasn't so much a hard and fast rule as it was a house custom turned into law.

For years whenever he arrived home from campus, he pressed the bell and Nira rushed to the door. She usually teased him from behind the closed door, saying funny things like, 'I'm sorry, handsome stranger. I can't let you in. My husband will be home any minute,' in a soft, purring tone.

Arif had no problem with this rule. He was so conditioned to it that opening the door of the house using his key felt made him feel he was burgling someone's home. Yet, Arif had broken this rule quite a few times over the past two or three weeks.

The last time he had broken it was the week before. He had come home early for the day. His sight was giving him headaches and nausea. Arif opened the door with his key and entered his silent house. He stepped into the family room as usual and scanned the room, wondering if his brain was playing tricks on him, but there was clearly no one there. As he stepped towards their bedroom he saw that the lights were on. He reached out and opened the door. His eyes met Nira's in an exchange of surprise and sadness. Nira and the girls were praying, raising their hands into the air, on top of two prayer mats spread across the bedroom floor. The younger daughter glanced over her shoulder and grinned at Arif but then got serious again and turned back to her prayers.

Arif walked back to the family room and sat on the sofa. He took off his glasses and let his head collapse backwards. The TV was turned off, but television gave him blurred vision and headaches anyway so Arif didn't mind. What he did mind was the silence.

That depressed silent environment sometimes seemed worse than death. Arif considered how an incident, or a terrible piece of news, could fragment a happy family and turn the family oasis into a desert. This was another horrifying side to cancer. The social inconvenience of it all and the toll on loved ones. Arif wondered if the sooner he was gone, the sooner the people he loved could heal and rise back to their former happy selves. The changes he had seen in Nira worried him the most. Her former healthy glow had completely dried up in just a few weeks and she had dark, puffy bags under her eyes.

In recent days, he had hardly seen Nira eat or drink. When he asked her if she had eaten, she would say she was fasting or that she had just broken her fast and had already eaten. Arif did not feel like eating either so he could relate.

For weeks he had sat at the dining table simply to maintain the family routine and the façade of normal life. All he wanted was for his girls, all three of them, to be normal and happy. But he knew there was no such thing as normal when it came to family life. The only thing normal about families was that they were dynamic and ever changing.

16

Amelia awoke and opened her eyes. The sun's feeble yellow glow filtered through her blinds as she kicked back the sheets and rolled out of bed. She bounced uncoordinatedly across the cold floor of her room to pull back the curtains and look outside. The air felt cold against her skin and there was condensation on the window. A glowing mist hung over everything in the garden.

She stepped quietly into the bathroom. It was a Sunday morning and she was wary of disturbing her housemates. Her face stared back at her through the mirror as she turned the tap and splashed her face with freezing cold water. The refreshment was instant. She turned on the shower which filled the room with plumes of steam. She waited for it to reach the perfect temperature before undressing and stepping inside.

She briefly lost all sense of time as the water washed over her head and down her body but was startled back into consciousness when furiously soaping herself and rinsing away the suds. She stood with eyes closed for a few more moments, before saying out loud, 'That's enough, Amelia. Get out.' Obediently, she turned off the taps and used her hand to flick water off her skin.

The sun had gone and the street was dark and grey by the time she had dressed and walked out the front door. Amelia marvelled at how quiet things were on Sunday mornings. The only sounds she could hear were the warbling of myna birds and a distant vehicle. Clouds of condensation formed in front of her as she laboured to breathe the cold, thick air.

Up ahead she saw a grey, concrete-rendered church, with young oak trees providing a lush perimeter. The massive red wooden doors were open, and she took a deep breath. She had never been inside a church. A visit to a Buddhist temple with her mother when she was a child, was her only experience of being inside a place of worship. She felt a pang of apprehension as she stood in front of the looming structure, ignorant about the customs and practices that went on inside.

As she walked up the stairs, a rotund pigeon scuttled out of her way, distracting her from the marvel of the steeply pitched roof and its red terracotta tiles.

The interior was dimly lit and the air felt colder than outside. Candles flickered on the walls, some of them real and others were vintage electrical impersonations. The static flickering added to the feeling that time had stopped. Downlights cast pins of illumination in strategic spots, brightening the corners of the room. A large crucifix took up the entire back wall. The place smelled of old incense, wax candles and the dust of time itself.

Amelia sighed. After spending Saturday afternoon deep in thought and questioning a God she'd never had any use for, she had found sleeping difficult. She tossed and turned as she thought of all the questions, complaints and contentious issues she wanted to raise with God, and a frustrated sadness built inside her as hot tears streamed across her face, evaporating before they could roll down any further.

She must have fallen asleep eventually because she found herself dreaming that she was massaging an old man who was seated in a big wooden chair in the middle of an expansive open field. The old man had long grey hair all over his naked body, which entangled her hands as she stood behind him, working on his shoulders and his neck. The old man groaned and chortled in a way that made her feel uncomfortable and dredged up degrading memories from the massage parlour. As his laughter hit a cackling crescendo, she noticed they were surrounded by a crowd of people who all joined in laughing. As they pointed at her, the skin around their faces began stretching towards the back of their skulls, exposing their teeth, and pulling their mouths into a sea of hideous grimaces.

Amelia shrieked. With no idea how to react, she turned back to the old man's shoulders and tried to double down on the massage as a way of ignoring the terrifying mob which had surrounded her. But as she glanced down in embarrassment, she realised that she was completely naked.

Amelia stopped massaging the man as she felt her ego and

autonomy dissolve into the horror all around her. As she froze, she looked at the crowd through her fringe in humiliation as they closed in around her chanting, 'Our turn next. Our turn next ...'

As they chanted, they ripped off their clothes, and when their clothes were gone, they continued ripping into their own flesh. Amelia felt tears rush down her cheeks as the people laughed and continued their encroachment. She searched in all directions for an escape route. Out of the corner of her eye she saw Arif's face in the back of the crowd. He was not laughing, but frantically shouting and waving his arms.

'Flee Amelia, flee,' he shouted.

'How can I flee? I'm surrounded,' Amelia shouted back.

Amelia felt the warm breath of the crowd against her skin and she suddenly smelled her own fear. The horrifying blur of gnashing teeth and angry eyes grew closer as a stinking fog swirled all around them.

Arif was still screaming, and Amelia started shrieking. The chanting grew louder and louder. When the crowd was almost within touching distance, Amelia tried to stretch her arms over the top of them, hoping she could reach Arif and he could pull her to safety. But this was impossible, even in the bizarre physics of her dream.

The noise was almost deafening. Amelia pushed against the ground with the heels of her feet, diving upwards into the ether. Her hands started to swim in a frenzied sort of breaststroke, lifting her upwards above the crowd. Suddenly, she heard and felt the world go '*Whoosh*' and she saw a blue butterfly rise from

Arif's hands. Then everything blurred around her as she shot over the heads of the people and became the wind itself.

She didn't look back, even though she had left Arif behind. She couldn't look back if she tried because when she looked ahead into the heavens, she saw she had become a perfect rocket shape. She was aerodynamic and sleek, and her head was locked in its perfect place. Everything around her was blue and still except for clouds of pure vapour that danced like seahorses all around her. The sounds of the unruly mob were far behind and the gentle breath of wind in her ears eased her into a calm meditative state.

Now, as she stood in the church facing a painting of Jesus surrounded by angels, Amelia felt the same feelings of serenity wash over her. She tried to pray but was very conscious of the fact that she didn't know how. Instead, she tried to remember the words she had rehearsed for the last two days in case she met an angel. But the words wouldn't come, and that made her feel weaker, unable to stand up. She drew her hands towards her chest and kneeled on the cold wooden floor. She stayed there for a few moments, her lips trembling and blubbing. When she felt more comfortable, she attempted to pray in her own crude way.

'Please Lord, do not take away the light of this man's life. This is a person who has given so much to my life, please do not snatch his away. If he dies, we will all lose, my Lord, and you will lose an angel on Earth. Please take my strength instead.'

Amelia sobbed loudly and her blurred vision created a stack of mirages that transcended time and space as she knelt on the floor with hands clasped, shivering in the cold empty church.

Arif sat in Bob Newsome's reception area with Nira by his side. He was trying to put on his bravest face and act as if everything was perfectly normal, but he knew he couldn't hide from his wife the fact that he felt terribly ill. He had noticed that she didn't seem able to fix her gaze on him for any amount of time at all these days. She would glance at him and then divert her vision, up or down, or anywhere else to avoid looking him in the eye. Even at home she seemed to be avoiding him and when she wasn't busy working around the house, she spent most of her time praying on her mat.

Arif watched Nira walk over to the water dispenser. She poured two drinks into disposable plastic cups from the tube attached to the machine. As she walked back Arif had trouble focusing and his eyes slowly closed and his head tilted slightly backwards.

'Are you sleeping, honey?' Nira softly asked.

'No. Just resting my eyes. Why?' Arif's eyes remained closed.

'Just asking. Sorry, my dear.'

Arif opened his eyes and tried gazing into Nira's, but she was looking at the cup of water she was about to pass him. He took the water.

'Thanks. But why are you saying sorry, my dear?' he asked grasping her free hand with his.

Nira withdrew her hand and folded her fingers into a fist that she held against her eyes. She started sobbing softly, her body jerking rhythmically.

'I'm sorry that you're suffering and I'm relatively healthy,' she said. 'I'm eating, sleeping, working …'

'Oh, Nira. Please don't be sorry.' Arif put his hand on Nira's lap. He smiled warmly. 'You've done so much for me. You're the best wife ever … How many husbands are as lucky as me? You've given me everything I could desire … serenity, expectation. The pride of being a father. Love, affection, care … everything. What else could you give?' he said.

Nira grabbed a hanky from her bag and dabbed her face, which was etched in pain.

'Arif, forgive me. I feel like I've been selfish for so long …' she sobbed.

'What could you possibly mean by selfishness?' he asked with genuine surprise.

'Maybe I could've reached deeper into your heart. You've achieved so much, but your lack of fulfilment, in your childhood, in your youth, in your whole life, I could've … I should've been more open, as your wife, to the depressed pain of your existence. Forgive me, Arif.'

Nira was crying uncontrollably and Arif shot an anxious glance at the receptionist. But she was seemingly in deep concentration, staring at her computer screen and oblivious to their drama. Nira diverted his gaze by looking him in the eye.

'When you're well, we'll go and visit the home country. We can meet with Azahar and Sayeed and we can all go to the banks of the river near the university and have a picnic. I will wear your favourite saree. The kids can play and we can ask Azahar and Sayeed to watch them while we walk barefoot along the bank of the river, alongside the *kashbon*, for hours and hours, holding hands, and when we get back to the kids, Azahar will be singing softly and the children will be asleep on the picnic blanket.'

She sighed.

'Doesn't that sound lovely, dear?'

Arif's eyes were wet and shiny as he looked at Nira.

'Yes, it does,' he said. 'It really does.'

Arif's head turned suddenly as the door to the doctor's office opened and someone walked out. He let his head drop as a sign of respect but more to avoid eye contact. He waited until the patient left the room before looking up and nodding as his eyes met the doctor's.

Arif noticed Nira was also looking at the doctor and felt her give his hand a gentle squeeze. Her face and mouth looked parched, but her eyes shone with a newfound sense of defiance that Arif recognised as being the real Nira. He returned the squeeze and prepared to stand up with a heavy heart that seemed to be weighing down his whole body.

'Mr and Mrs Ahmed, good to see you,' Bob Newsome said exuding a profound sense of calm. 'Please follow me.'

Arif found his face impossible to read, like a poker player on late night television, but benevolent.

Arif stood and detected a slight resistance in Nira's hand. As he pulled her gently towards the office, he felt a slight tremble.

They sat in front of the doctor's desk. Transparencies of the MRI were visible on the light box. The surgeon spoke to them both, but Arif was having trouble listening. He heard occasional words like 'brain surgery', 'radiotherapy', and 'chemotherapy', but they mostly washed over him. They were meaningless. He could feel Nira's gaze on the side of his head and registered that she was crying uncontrollably, as their youngest child would.

The sound of pounding rain drifted down from the roof and Arif turned to look out the window. There were dense black clouds and the rain was teeming down.

He remembered the monsoons in the village where he was born, and wondered if nature and a mother's love were both forms of the same life force. In the same way a mother felt a child's joys and pains, did Mother Nature do the same? He decided it didn't matter. Everything was a construct. He considered the rain and imagined it as tears as he thought about it soaking into the earth and providing life with the solvent it needed to exist.

Amelia looked at her watch and glanced around the seminar room of the science faculty, which had been decorated with school banners as soft classical music played over the public address system. The program was soon due to start and a light murmur filled the room. She didn't feel like mingling with the other guests, most of whom looked completely new to her. It was as if she was the only undergraduate student there. She glanced at the entrance in hope and expectation. Her heart was beating fast.

The dean of the faculty stepped in front of the podium and began a speech, the first of the night. Amelia was too distracted to take in what he was saying. She stared at the door, hoping

Arif would saunter into the room, in good spirits and good health.

The dean called her name and she watched Professor McCullum walk on to the podium as the dean invited her to take her place next to them, but none of it registered. It was only when her name was called again that her brain kicked back into action and she walked up the aisle towards them. Professor McCullum took the microphone.

'On behalf of the dean, the faculty and the entire university I'd like to present Yameli Nguyen, whom we all know as Amelia, with the Dean's Award of Excellence for getting an almost perfect score in all the subjects she's attempted. Congratulations, Amelia. You've made us all proud. We wish you all the best for all your future endeavours.'

The audience started clapping as Professor McCullum shook her hand and presented her with an envelope and a beautiful academic award in a black frame.

Amelia's eyes were filled with tears. The dean leaned forward whispered in her ear. 'Don't cry, Amelia; just look at the camera and give us a big smile. Congratulations, you're a credit to yourself and this entire university.'

Amelia took another quick glance at the door and let out a loud cry.

Amelia stood outside the massage parlour and shook her head. Why had she come back? She swore that she would never return, yet here she was on the footpath outside, with her hand raised, pushing the door open.

She heard the familiar chiming of the crystal curtain as she entered with gritted teeth. There was a time when that shimmering sound would fill her heart with dread, as she wondered what sort of monster might be in the lobby, waiting for her 'services'. But not all her clients were bad, she reminded herself. Some were basically decent but lonely men, who had no other outlet for human touch, and some were like Arif...

The musty smell of incense and stale massage oil hit her in the nose, and she grimaced as the door behind the reception desk opened and she saw Ms Maliwan standing in the dim, gloomy light with a bemused smile on her face.

Ms Maliwan greeted her with eyes showing surprise and a sarcastic lilt to her voice. 'You've returned, Amelia. I didn't expect to see you again. What business do you have coming back to my shop?'

'Hi, Ms Maliwan. I'm not sure why I'm here, to be honest.'

Amelia paused for a moment, deep in thought. 'I'm going home next week, back to my own country. I don't know many people here and I guess I came back for a sense of closure.'

'Have you finished your studies? Are you going home for good?'

'I'm not sure yet. I feel homesick and I miss my family. I haven't seen them for such a long time.'

Ms Maliwan stood with hands on her hips, staring straight through Amelia, as she looked around the lobby, storing it up in her memory.

'Is Ella here today?' Amelia asked.

'No, she isn't. Ella's no longer here. I can't tell you where she is because I don't know,' Ms Maliwan snapped.

Amelia sighed as Ms Maliwan looked at her somewhat suspiciously.

'Is everything all right, Amelia? You don't look well. Do you need to sit down?'

Ms Maliwan's voice showed genuine concern.

'Do you mind if I have a look in my old room? Just for old time's sake.'

'You're a strange girl, Amelia.' The older woman shook her head, puzzled. 'Of course you can. Millie doesn't start for another hour or so. Feel free to stay there if you need to. You can even lie down but come and fetch me before you leave.'

Amelia thanked Ms Maliwan and walked through the door that led to her old studio. She thought of Arif as she stepped through the white curtain and instantly felt numb when she saw the massage table and the old chair where the men stacked their clothes. A sudden pain hit her in the stomach and her mouth became bitter with the taste of bile. She hurried back to the lobby.

'I'm sorry Ms Maliwan. I need to go. You were right, I'm not feeling well.'

Ms Maliwan looked up from behind the reception counter with a weary face.

'Goodbye, Amelia. All the best. I hope I never see you in this shop again, my dear,' she said.

Amelia said goodbye and plunged out the door and into the fresh air. The day was overcast and looked like it might drizzle. It was the perfect example of what locals called a gloomy day.

Amelia decided to take a bus to the university. When she got there, the campus was nearly empty and the bird song was louder than usual. There were a few older, postgraduate research students in the cafeteria and out the front of the library as she walked past, but the usual buzz of younger students was missing and the place felt sedate without it.

The entire campus became a lonely, lifeless arena during vacation. Nature seemed to take over in the outdoor areas, where the trees and grass seemed greener and there were birds everywhere, especially on the lawns. They occasionally looked up at her but went back to picking the ground and overturning sods as she walked past.

Amelia entered the science building and walked languidly down the old corridor she knew so well. Her black bag swung on her shoulder. The squeak of her bag's brass strap ends sounded deafening in the near silence all around her. She walked through a gentle curve in the corridor that was a sign that her destination was near. She paused for a moment exactly where she often used to stop.

Amelia took a deep breath and walked past Arif's office. The doors were closed. It seemed to be locked and there was no light coming from inside. She didn't linger but continued along the rest of the corridor, making her exit through the doorway at the end.

The clouds had become heavier and darker and her hair was blowing in the wind. walked across the green oval Amelia glanced at the library building, thinking about how well she had been treated when she worked there. She walked past the bench where the smokers would congregate. Despite the wind, everything seemed frozen.

She stopped and sat on the smokers' bench for the first time, looking first at the cigarette butts that had killed the grass around them and then at the vast expanse of green that unfolded before her. The oval seemed huge and the birds seemed so small.

Amelia was aware that she felt empty inside, as if her heart had stopped beating. Her lower lip began to tremble.

It's just the cold, she told herself.

Amelia thought of Arif. She hoped she would see him again, and that when she returned to her studies, he'd be back on campus, healthy once more. They could sit in the library and he could show her how to write quality research papers. Then they'd go to the cafeteria for tea and coffee and laugh at each other's jokes without a worry in the world. She glanced over to where she remembered eating lamb chops and sausages, sitting on the grass, with so many possibilities. Perhaps one day they would meet for lunch, chatting in a restaurant, off campus. This time, Amelia would pay the bill.

Tears poured down her face and she noticed globules of moisture on the tips of the grass all around her. It suddenly seemed like she was in a swamp, and then as if the world was a swamp. The oval wasn't there anymore, only green swamp water.

Amelia struggled to her feet and trudged away from the bare earth of the smoking area and lay down on the grass. She wanted to sink slowly into the marshy water she could see all around her. The wind blew and the blades of grass around her ears shook gently as she heard the sound of a butterfly's wings and a deep sonorous voice singing softly into her ear.

You'll come a-waltzing Matilda with me ....